Dig up the flowers?

Hey, she'd spent most of the afternoon *planting* those flowers, working in the hot afternoon sun. I'd sat right there beside and watched the whole thing. It made absolutely no sense ...

"Hank, do as you're told!" Again, it was her voice.

My gaze leaped around, looking for her. Where was she? I'd heard her voice, loud and clear, but saw no sign of her. Did I dare enter her yard and begin the process of ...

Oooo boy, this didn't sound right. I mean, it sounded crazy. Dig up her flowers? For a moment, I was paralyzed. For one of the few times in my career, I had no idea what I should do.

The Case of the Mysterious Voice

John R. Erickson

Illustrations by Gerald L. Holmes

PUFFIN BOOKS
An Imprint of Penguin Group (USA) Inc.

PUFFIN BOOKS

Published by the Penguin Group

Penguin Young Readers Group, 345 Hudson Street, New York, New York 10014, U.S.A.

Penguin Group (Canada), 90 Eglinton Avenue East, Suite 700,
Toronto, Ontario, Canada M4P 2Y3 (a division of Pearson Penguin Canada Inc.)

Penguin Books Ltd, 80 Strand, London WC2R 0RL, England

Penguin Ireland, 25 St Stephen's Green, Dublin 2, Ireland (a division of Penguin Books Ltd)

Penguin Group (Australia), 250 Camberwell Road, Camberwell, Victoria 3124, Australia
(a division of Pearson Australia Group Pty Ltd)

Penguin Books India Pvt Ltd, 11 Community Centre,
Panchsheel Park, New Delhi - 110 017, India

Penguin Group (NZ), 67 Apollo Drive, Rosedale, Auckland 0632, New Zealand
(a division of Pearson New Zealand Ltd)

Penguin Books (South Africa) (Pty) Ltd, 24 Sturdee Avenue,
Johannesburg 2196, South Africa

Registered Offices: Penguin Books Ltd, 80 Strand, London WC2R 0RL, England

Published simultaneously in the United States of America by
Viking Children's Books and Puffin Books,
divisions of Penguin Young Readers Group, 2011

1 3 5 7 9 10 8 6 4 2

CIP DATA IS AVAILABLE UPON REQUEST

Puffin Books ISBN 978-0-14-241981-6

Hank the Cowdog® is a registered trademark of John R. Erickson.
Printed in the United States of America

Dedicated to the memory of Soren Dahlstrom.

CONTENTS

The Case of the
Mysterious Voice

CHAPTER ONE

Sally May Plans
a Picnic

It's me again, Hank the Cowdog. The mystery began on a Friday morning in May, as I recall. Yes, I'm sure it was May, because we'd finished branding our spring calves and were enjoying a period of quiet before hay season started.

Loper and Slim were sitting in lawn chairs in the backyard, drinking coffee and enjoying the cool of the morning. It was something they didn't do very often. Drover and I had finished our morning patrol and had assembled at the yard gate. There, we watched and listened.

Loper said, "It sure is peaceful out here."

"Yep."

"Every once in a while, a man needs to slow down and notice the wonders of God's creation."

"Yep. When do you reckon that'll start?"

Loper gave him a stern look. "Right now. That's what we're doing. We had a hard week getting the branding done, and now we can relax a little bit."

Slim took a slurp of coffee. "Okay with me."

Loper filled his lungs with fresh air and looked up at the sky. "For the next two days, I'm going to stick around the house—help Sally May with the yard work and take care of those little fix-up jobs that always seem to get put off. I might even take Alfred fishing."

Slim flashed a grin. "I've heard this before."

"Oh yeah? Well, you just watch. A man needs to stop and smell the roses."

"Loper, you wouldn't know a rose from a dandelion ... and speaking of dandelions, you've got a bunch of 'em growing in your yard. I'll loan you my pocketknife if you want to start digging 'em up right now."

"Thanks. I've got my own knife, and I'll put dandelions on my list of things to do."

"That's just what I figured."

Loper shook his head and muttered something under his breath. "Slim, do you know what your biggest problem is?"

"Poverty."

"No. You have a sour attitude about your fellow man."

"Not all of 'em, just the ones I know."

"Five bucks says that I spend the next two days doing chores around the house."

"I hate to take money from a fool."

Loper snapped his fingers. "Step up, son. We know you've got the mouth. Do you have five dollars to back it up?"

Sim dug out his wallet and peeked inside. "Yes, I do, and I think I'm fixing to double it."

"You're fixing to *lose* it, and when you do, I don't want to hear you whine and moan. A deal's a deal."

Slim bobbed his head in agreement. "A deal's a deal."

At that very moment, the back door opened and out stepped . . . oops. Sally May. All at once, I felt . . . you know, sometimes when she shows up, I'm seized by terrible feelings of guilt. It's as though I've done something naughty and she *knows it*.

She has these eyes that can penetrate skin and bones, don't you know, and she can see right into the gizzardly depths of a dog's soul. But the crazy thing was that, on that particular morning, my soul was as clean and pure as freshly fallen snow.

3

I hadn't done anything wrong! I hadn't even *thought* about doing anything wrong, and yet ...

Before I even had a chance to think about it, I slipped into a program we call Leaving Town. I mean, it happened in a split second and without even thinking about it, I began creeping for the nearest exit.

But then I noticed an important detail: Sally May wore a radiant smile. If she'd picked up any Naughty Signals from me, she wouldn't have been smiling.

I stopped slinking away and heaved a sigh of relief. "Drover, she seems to be in a good mood this morning."

He had been staring off into space, and his eyes drifted down to me. "Oh, hi. What's good mud?"

"Good mud? Well, when you add good moisture to common dirt, you get good mud, and good mud is good for the plants and flowers."

"I love it when the grass is green and the wild-flowers bloom."

"Yes, and we've had a nice spring, haven't we?"

"Yeah, if I could just get rid of these allergies." He sneezed. "By dose gids stobbed ubb all the tibe." He sneezed again. "See whud I beed?"

"Yes, I see what you mean. I'm sorry you're having trouble."

"Thags."

"You're welcome." There was a moment of silence. "Drover, you said something about 'good mud.' Was there some special reason why you wanted to talk about mud this morning? I have no objections, but it seems a little odd. Have you been worrying about mud?"

He gave that some thought. "Well, mud's always muddy."

"That's true, good point. Does it bother you that mud is muddy?"

"Not really. I don't think about mud very often."

"Yes, and that's my whole point. Most of us go through entire weeks and months without thinking about mud, yet you brought up the subject."

"I did?"

"You certainly did. You asked my opinion about good mud."

His eyes blanked out. "I'll be derned. What did you say?"

"I said ... never mind. Why did you bring up the subject of mud in the first place?"

"Well, let me think." He scowled and rolled his eyes around. "Wait, I just remembered. You said Sally May found some good mud."

I took a deep breath and looked up at the sky.

"Drover, please pay attention. I said that Sally May appears to be in a good *mood*."

"I'll be derned. I wonder why."

"I was trying to listen so that I could find out, but you started blabbering about mud. Stop talking about mud."

"Sorry." He sneezed. "Gosh, baby I'be allergig to bud."

"You're not allergic to mud, but you might be losing your marbles."

"I doed have any barbles."

"Maybe that's it."

Drover does this all the time, you know. He pulls me into a conversation and all at once, I realize that nobody has any idea what we're talking about. Sometimes I think . . . never mind.

I left him alone with his runny nose and turned my attention back to the house, just in time to hear Sally May exclaim, "I have an exciting announcement to make."

Slim and Loper sat up and looked at her. Loper said, "Oh?"

She clapped her hands together. "I've invited the church choir out for a picnic tomorrow. While I go to town and shop for groceries, you boys can mow and rake and clean up the yard. Oh, and

7

we've got a bunch of dandelions in the front yard."

Sally May didn't notice the dead silence that had fallen over the cowboy crowd, but I did. Loper's eyes darted around for a moment, then he glanced at his watch and stood up.

"Hon, that sounds great, but I've got an appointment with the accountant at nine. I'd better get moving. Give Slim a list of things to do."

Sally May went back into the house, leaving Slim and Loper alone. Slim's face had turned to cement. "Loper, most people think you're a low-down skunk. Not me. I think you're worse than that."

"Don't take it personally. I really do need to talk to the accountant."

"Yeah, and it's odd that you didn't think about it until your wife pulled out the Honey-Do List."

Loper shrugged. "We all have our gifts and talents. You're better at yard work than I am."

"How would you know? The last time you did any yard work, you were in the third grade."

Loper cackled. "You know, hardship seems to bring out your sense of humor. By this afternoon, you'll be right up there with Mark Twain."

Slim leaned forward and glared at him. "Hey Loper, I hired onto this outfit as a *cowboy*.

Remember cowboys? They do things with a horse and a catch-rope."

Loper tossed down the last swig of coffee. "Well, you were never much good at either one, so we're trying to find little jobs to keep you out of trouble. I'll get back as soon as I can."

Loper headed for the house. Slim's glare followed him. "I know you will. Hey, aren't you forgetting something?"

Loper stopped and turned around. "What?"

Slim stuck out his hand. "Five bucks, buddy. A deal's a deal."

Loper came back, dug his wallet out of his hip pocket, and laid a five-dollar bill across Slim's palm. "Slim, that's the best five bucks I ever spent. Be happy in your work."

Whistling a tune, Loper went into the house. Slim remained in his chair for another minute, fuming in silence.

CHAPTER TWO

Alfred's
Great Idea

Yes, old Slim was in a bad mood, still fuming when Loper drove away in his pickup. He was in such a high snit, we dogs had to activate the Sharing of Pain. Following our procedures, we went into Mournful Eyes, Sad Ears, and Dead Tail.

It seemed to be working, and I think we had him going in the right direction, when Sally May and Baby Molly came out, dressed up for their trip to the grocery store, and Sally May gave him her list of things to do.

It was a long list, and my impression was that Slim didn't enjoy reading it. Then Sally May said, "Oh, and I think I'll let Alfred stay with you.

There's nothing for him to do in town, and maybe he can help."

Slim stared at her. "Oh good."

Alfred said, "Mom, I wanted to go to town."

"Nevertheless," she kissed him on the cheek, "you'll stay and help Slim."

Moments later, she drove away, leaving the four of us (me, Drover, Slim, and Alfred) standing in a cloud of dust and a heavy silence. The silence grew heavier by the second and, when nobody spoke, I felt the need to whap my tail on the ground.

It's a gesture we use in awkward moments, don't you see, and sometimes it helps to remove some of the explosive vapors from the air.

The boy had Pout written all over his face. "I don't like working in the dumb old yard."

Slim grumbled, "It's genetic, son."

"What does that mean?"

"Never mind. Come back in ten years and I'll explain it." He headed for the machine shed, and we followed. "For now, here's all you need to know. At Slim's Day Care Service, we have a short list of rules: Don't make noise, don't get in the way, don't make a mess, and most of all, don't ask a bunch of questions."

"My mom says it's good to ask questions."

"Yeah, well, your mom ain't here."

"Is it okay if I breathe?"

"If you're quiet, one breath every hour."

"What if I faint?"

"You'll get eaten up by red ants."

"They eat little boys?"

"All the time."

"Are you teasing?"

"Heck no. Them ants would rather eat a little boy than a bowl of ice cream."

"Can we have some ice cream?"

"No."

"I'm hungry."

"Take your troubles to the Lord. I don't care."

We continued walking toward the machine shed. "Hey, Swim?"

"What."

"Can I throw the cat in the stock tank?"

Slim stopped and looked down at the boy. "Now, why would you want to do that?"

Alfred shrugged. "He needs a bath. And I'm bored."

"Bored, huh? Well, boredom's a sure path to knowledge. Most usually, when a cat gets a bath, a boy gets an education."

"So it's okay?"

Slim laid a hand on his shoulder. "My advice

is, find something else to do. Now, if you'll excuse me ..."

Slim trudged on down to the machine shed to fetch the lawn mower. Alfred turned to us with ... well, you'd have to call it a wicked little grin, and whispered, "Come on, doggies, let's give Pete a bath!"

Well, you talk about something that will brighten your day! The dark clouds just seemed to roll away and all at once, we had Sunshine Forever. What a great idea! I was surprised that I hadn't thought of it myself. Hey, when times are hard and troubles are getting you down, happiness is just around the corner.

All you need is an annoying ranch cat and a tank full of water.

Ho ho, hee hee, ha ha.

I loved it!

We headed down to the yard, knowing exactly where we would find Mister Never Sweat: in the iris patch on the north side of the house. That's where he spent most of his time in the summer, loafing and lounging and lurking in the shade. He came out only for special occasions, such as to mooch my supper scraps or to rub on Sally May's ankles.

As you might recall, Sally May didn't allow

dogs in her yard, but Pete? He was her Precious Kitty, and the little fraud had free run of the whole ranch. He could go anywhere and do anything and...

Have I mentioned that I don't like cats? I don't like cats, never have, just don't get along with 'em at all. Show me a cat and I'll find a place to park him—up the nearest tree.

Or in the nearest stock tank. Hee hee. Boy, this was going to be great! You know about cats and water, right? They hate water! I was so excited, I was trembling all over.

At last, we arrived at the yard gate. Alfred turned to us dogs and brought a finger to his lips. "Shh. I'll go find him. Y'all wait right here, 'cause dogs can't come in the yard."

Right. It was a silly rule, but there was nothing we could do about it.

We dogs waited outside the yard, while Alfred headed for the iris patch, trying to look as innocent as an ornery little stinkpot could look.

Drover turned to me. "What are we doing now?"

"Don't you ever listen?"

"Oh... sometimes. Did I miss something?"

"Yes. Alfred's looking for the cat."

"Oh good. Pete's a nice kitty."

"Yes, and we're going to give him a nice bath."

Drover's eyes widened. "A bath? Cats hate water."

"I doubt that Alfred will ask his opinion."

"Gosh, you mean . . ." Drover thought about that for a moment, then a silly grin rippled across his mouth. "Oh, I get it now. Hee hee. We're going to throw the cat into the stock tank?"

"That's correct. Very good. Now hush and watch the show. This is going to be fun."

We concentrated on the scene in the yard. Alfred walked along the side of the house, peeking into all the shrubs and flowers and searching for an unemployed cat. No luck. But then he came to the corner of the house and peeked into the iris patch.

His face bloomed into a grin. He'd located our pigeon . . . uh, the cat, let us say, right where I had predicted he would be, loafing in the shade. But then the lad made a mistake. He said, "Hi Pete, nice kitty, come here. Kitty kitty kitty."

Did you catch his mistake? He forgot to use Backwards Logic. See, any time you want to catch a cat, you should tell him to buzz off or run away, then he'll come scampering toward you and start rubbing on your legs. You won't be able to run fast enough to get away from him.

But call him a "nice kitty" and tell him "come

here," and he'll do just what Pete did, flatten his ears and start oozing away. Alfred had to chase him all the way around to the front of the house and drag him out from under a cedar bush.

But the important thing was that we got him captured, and soon we were heading down to the corrals. Alfred carried him, and I could see that Pete was beginning to smell a rat.

"Where are we going, Hankie?"

"Oh, we thought it might be fun to do some exploring."

"Hmmm. And what are we going to explore?"

"You never know, Pete. Maybe we'll climb the haystack or catch turtles."

His cunning little eyes moved from side to side. "Hmm. Those aren't things that cats do, Hankie, and I'm wondering why I was invited."

"Well, I guess Little Alfred got to feeling sorry for you. Let's face it, Pete. You have no personality and no friends. You need help with your social life."

"Oh really."

"Yes, it's a common trait in cats. Oh, and we've noticed that you live an unhealthy lifestyle. You never do anything, Pete, and to be perfectly honest, you're getting a little overweight. I hate to be the one to tell you, but it's true. You need some exercise."

Alfred opened a wooden gate and we entered the corrals. Pete had begun twitching the last inch of his tail, a sure sign that his scheming little mind had kicked into high gear.

"You know, Hankie, I'm not fond of exercise."

"I know you're not, but sometimes you need to play with your friends."

"But Hankie, you said I don't have any friends."

"I said that? Ha ha. Well, the truth leaks out, doesn't it?"

"So ... I'm going to get some exercise, climbing the haystack?"

We had reached the stock tank. I turned a big smile on Kitty Kitty. "Exactly. Or here's another idea. Had you ever considered ... swimming?"

Hee hee. I had just let the cat out of the sandbox. Sandbag.

Out of the bag, let us say. I had just let the cat out of the bag.

Bathing
the Cat

Okay, we need to have a little talk. We know each other pretty well, right? And you're aware that I'm not fond of admitting mistakes, right? Well, what would you think if I told you that I made ... that is, what would you think if I announced ... This is really tough, so let's come at it from another angle, and this time I'm just going to blurt it out.

I shouldn't have uttered the word "swimming" in the presence of the cat.

There, it's all out in the open and now you're ready to hear the second piece of bad news. Our plans for the cat blew up like a can of hair spray in a burning garbage barrel, and fellers, it happened so fast, none of us saw it coming.

Okay, let's take a deep breath and reset the stage. There we were, Alfred and Drover and I, standing on the cement in front of the stock tank, and Alfred was cuddling Mister Kitty Precious in his arms. All three of us were quivering with antiseptic and trying to bite back our grins, for you see . . .

Wait, hold everything. We weren't quivering with *antiseptic*. Antiseptic is that stuff you dump on a cut or wound. It kills creepy little bugs that can make your finger swell up and eat your liver, and that's why mommies run for the medicine cabinet when little children get cuts, scratches, and aberrations.

Abrasions, there we go. Aberrations are something else, and they don't require anything you might find in a medicine cabinet.

Words are interesting, aren't they? I kind of enjoy playing around with 'em.

Now, where were we?

I have no idea. Huh.

Seems to me that we were talking about something pretty exciting, but all at once . . . boy, one second you can be as focused as a laser bean, and the next, everything just goes to seed.

Wait. Beans are seeds, right? Maybe that's a

clue that we were discussing seeds. Okay, here we go. Your average ranch in the Texas Panhandle has a whole bunch of weeds and plants, and every year they produce about ten zillion seeds. We have your grass seeds, your milkweed seeds, your cottonwood seeds, and your wildflower seeds.

We have other objects on the ranch that never make seeds, such as your rocks, your fence posts, and your ... Wait, we weren't talking about seeds.

This is frustrating. Could I have been talking about Miss Beulah? Maybe so, because ... well, I won't say that I think about her all the time, but several times during the course of an average day, I find myself staring at her picture on the bookshelf of my mind.

Refined nose, gorgeous eyes, perfect ears. What a woman! But you look into those deep, intelligent eyes and you wonder ... HOW COULD SHE LOVE A BIRD DOG? If she's so smart, why can't she figure out ...

Wait, hold everything. The cat. We were about to launch the cat into the stock tank, remember? Try to work on your concentration, and please don't interrupt me again.

Okay, now we're cooking. There we stood at the edge of a stock tank full of stinking moss-water, trying our best to keep from laughing out loud, because we knew what was coming next.

Hee hee. Kitty would go flying into the tank and we would enjoy several minutes of good, wholesome family entertainment.

But before that could happen, I made a ... before that could happen, Drover made one of the dumbest mistakes he'd ever made. He said (and this is a direct quote), he asked the cat, "Have you ever considered swimming?"

Oh brother. I couldn't believe my ears. Of all the bone-headed things he could have said! Do you have any idea what happens to a cat when you mention swimming?

A lot. Within mere seconds, Kitty transformed into a helicopter, a buzz saw, a meat grinder, a hissing, yowling explosion of arms, legs, paws, and nasty little cat-claw razors.

He gave Little Alfred the scratching of his young life, and then the little lunatic ... I'm not going to tell you what else he did.

I mean, there are some things we can report and some things that ... uh ... need to be shielded from public scrutiny, shall we say. Our main concern is the little children, no kidding. How would they respond if they ever found out that one of

their heroes got buzz sawed by a rinky-dink little ranch cat?

It could have a terrible effect. They might not be able to sleep for weeks. They might forget to brush their teeth. Some of them might make puddles in the bed. We just can't risk it, and that's why you will find a big hole in the middle of this story.

I'm sorry to take such extreme measures, but our Security Division has pretty strict rules about this stuff. You'll never know all the details of this case, because we've slapped Top Secret on all those files and they'll stay in the vault for two hundred years.

Please don't whine about it. Believe me, you don't want to hear all the grizzly details.

But the port we can repair . . . the part we can report, let us say, is that Little Alfred gained important information about bathing cats: *It's something you might not want to try very often.* I mean, he had red marks on one cheek, both arms, both hands, and the left side of his neck.

And what about the villain? Well, after I finally got him off the back of my neck . . . hold it! Forget I said that. It's classified and we could get in big trouble. I said nothing about a DELETED on the back of my DELETED.

What I meant to say was that the hateful little mutter-mumble hit the ground and set sail for the house, but you'll be proud to know that I seized this opportunity to strike a blow for children and dogs all across America.

I leaped into my Rocket Dog suit (lucky I'd brought it along), and twisted the Blast Dial all the way to the right. The Portable Rocket Engine Backpack (PREB) kicked in and I chased the cat all the way back to the yard.

There, I removed my flight helmet and yelled, "And that's what you get for scratching innocent children! If you ever do it again, I'll do it againer!"

Pretty impressive, huh? You bet. I got him told.

You might be wondering, "Where was Drover while all this was going on?" Great question. At the first sign of trouble, he just vanished, and we're talking about "poof," like a puff of smoke in a tornado.

But never mind. I caught up with Little Alfred. He was heading for the house in a fast walk. It was kind of a touching scene, a boy and his dog, marching home after a big triumph on the field of . . . okay, we didn't have much to celebrate, might as well be honest about it. We'd been ambushed by a sniveling, scheming little buzz saw of a cat. I was embarrassed about it, and Alfred had collected enough scratches to last him for six months.

We weren't feeling too proud of ourselves is the point. In fact, Alfred's lower lip was stuck out so far, I was afraid he might step on it.

We found Slim in the backyard, pushing a gasoline-powered lawn mower and dripping sweat, and looking permanently mad about it. When he saw us coming, he shut off the mower, mopped his brow on his shirtsleeve, and looked down at Alfred.

"Good honk, what got a-holt of you?"

The boy was so mad, he was about to cry. "The dumb old cat scwatched me! Look." He pointed to the red lines on his cheeks.

Slim studied the marks and laid a hand on the boy's shoulder. "Son, you've had a little brush with something called 'education.'" He leaned down and lowered his voice. "When you try to throw a live cat into the water, he'll scratch you—not every *other* time, but every time. Now, you ought to feel proud, 'cause Pete just raised your IQ about twenty points."

Alfred's lip was still pooched out. "Can you put some medicine on my scwatches?"

"Sure, come on."

Slim went slouching toward the yard gate, and Alfred said, "Hey, Swim, the medicine's in the house."

"Mine ain't. It's in the machine shed. Come on."

Hmm. That seemed odd, but we followed him up the hill to the machine shed. Inside, he selected a gallon jug with big black letters that said, KEROSENE. He found a grease rag that was halfway clean, dumped some kerosene on it, and dabbed it on Alfred's wounds.

The lad's eyes grew wide. "Hey, that burns!"

Slim nodded. "Yes sir, coal oil's the best medicine you can buy. Shucks, it'll even cure a cough if you drink it with some sugar."

"Yeah, but it stinks!"

"Too bad. By grabs, when you hang out with a cowboy, you get cowboy cures. If that don't suit you, find another babysitter. Now, leave the cat alone and let me get back to . . ."

At that moment, we heard a vehicle pull up in front of the machine shed. You'll never guess who it was, so I'll tell you. No, maybe I won't. If I told, it might scare you, and then nobody would read the next chapter.

I guess you'll have to keep on reading.

CHAPTER FOUR

The Police Arrive

Are you still with me? Good. Grab hold of something solid.

It was Chief Deputy Sheriff Bobby Kile. Uh-oh. When the deputy sheriff shows up, it usually means trouble.

When he stepped out of his car, Slim said, "Now, Bobby, if this is about that last overdraft on my bank account..."

The deputy laughed. "Don't worry. I was just passing through the country and thought I'd stop by and see how y'all are doing."

"Well, we're hot and dry, and I've been demoted to yard boy and babysitter." He jerked his thumb toward Alfred. "Me and Button were just having a seminary on cats and water."

The deputy narrowed his eyes and studied Alfred's face. "What happened?"

"Well, he offered to give the cat a bath, and I guess old Pete took a dim view of that."

The deputy nodded. "Cats." His gaze wandered to the horizon and he jingled some coins in his pocket. "Slim, you ever own a parrot?"

"A parrot? Nope."

"You ever wish you owned a parrot?"

"Not even in my wildest dreams. Why?"

The deputy gestured toward his car. "Well, I've got one and I need to sell him."

Slim chuckled. "How in thunder did you end up with a parrot?"

"Two weeks ago, a guy from Oklahoma missed a turn and drove his pickup into Debbie Barnett's kitchen. I answered the call and when I got there, he was still sitting in the pickup, with a parrot on his shoulder."

Slim was grinning. "How'd he happen to drive into Debbie's kitchen?"

"Well, he'd stayed too long at the beer joint and he was 'impaired,' as we say. He'll be in jail for quite a spell, and I ended up with his bird."

"How's that working out?"

Deputy Kile pulled on his chin. "Slim, people

pay thousands of dollars for a bird like Dink, but I'm going to make someone a special deal."

"Uh huh. Who'd you have in mind?"

"I'll sell you the bird, the perch, and twenty pounds of feed for fifty bucks. What do you say?"

"I don't have fifty bucks. If I did, I'd quit this yard job and go cowboying."

"Ten?"

"Nope."

"All right, let's cut to the chase." The deputy's smile faded. "I've had to share my office with that idiot parrot, and he's driving me crazy. He talks all the time and he's a troublemaker. If I can't find a home for him, he's liable to end up as filler in a chicken pot pie."

"Bobby, I'd like to help, but I just don't have any use for a bird."

"What about Loper?"

Silence. I could almost see the wheels turning in Slim's mind. His eyes brightened and a smile bloomed on his mouth. "You know, he's always wanted a parrot."

"No kidding?"

"Why, this very morning as we were drinking coffee in the yard, he talked about how he wished someone would give him a parrot for Father's Day."

Deputy Kile's face burst into a broad smile. "Well, brother, we can fix him up!"

He moved with uncommon speed, opened the back door of his squad car, and brought out a wooden perch with three legs. Five minutes later, the perch and the bird had been relocated on the back porch.

Slim walked the deputy back to his car. "What keeps him from flying away?"

"I don't know, but you can't pry him off that perch."

"You said something about him being a troublemaker?"

They had reached the deputy's car, and Officer Kile was wearing an odd smile. "Slim, that bird's a genius. Once he hears a voice, he can reproduce it like a tape recorder. You have no idea ..." He started laughing and didn't finish his sentence.

When he drove away, Alfred looked up at Slim. "I didn't know my dad wanted a parrot."

"Yes, well, he didn't know it either, but I think he'll be thrilled."

Alfred gave his head a shake. "That doesn't sound like my dad."

Chuckling to himself, Slim went back to his mowing and put Alfred to work picking up sticks and branches in the yard. Me? I figured I might as well meet the new bird and give him a little introduction to life on my ranch.

It's something we try to do any time a rookie shows up on the place. We call it "orientation," and we've found that ten minutes of good orientation can save days of trouble on the other end.

I swaggered up to the yard gate and studied the new guy. He was big for a bird, about the size of your average pigeon, but with a long tail, a huge curved beak, weird reddish eyes, and feathers that had every color in the rainbow: red, green, yellow, and orange. He stood on the wooden perch, cocked his head, and stared at me with one of those weird eyes.

"My name is Hank the Cowdog. I'm head of the ranch's Security Division. I handle cattle, special crimes, sun bark-up, postal employees, and a lot of other stuff that's none of your business. I'm here to welcome you to my ranch."

I began pacing, as I often do when I have an important message to deliver. "That said, let's forget the niceties and go straight to the point. You're the new guy on the ranch. You're also a bird. I don't like either one, so your stay with us is not likely to be much fun. I don't care.

"Now, let's go over the rules. We have a few simple ones. The first rule is, *this is my ranch.* Nothing happens out here without my permission. Period. The second, third, and fourth rules are, *keep your mouth shut.* Any questions so far?"

The bird blinked his red eye and began using his beak to scratch under his left wing. "Hey, you, Dink! Stand at attention when you're being addressed by a superior officer!" The bird stopped scratching. "That's better. Our fifth rule is, *no scratching of any kind during orientation.* Scratch on your own time."

I turned and looked off to the west. Sure enough, Drover was peeking his head out of the machine shed. Just as I figured, he'd been watching. "Drover? Come here! Immediately." I turned back to the bird. "I want to introduce you to my assistant, Drover C. Dog. He's a goof-off, but in my absence, you will take orders from him."

Drover arrived just then, wearing his usual silly grin. "Oh, hi. What's that?"

"That is a parrot. Where were you when I was being shredded by the cat?"

"What cat? Oh, you mean down at the stock tank?"

"That's correct. Answer the question."

"Well, let me think." He rolled his eyes around. "I guess I left."

I gave him a withering glare. "I guess you did. Your commanding officer had been ambushed by a deranged cat, and you ran from the field of battle."

"Yeah, the noise was hurting my ears."

"Hurting your ears! Do you have any idea what was happening to *my* ears? That cat was trying to tear them off my head! Thirteen Chicken Marks, Drover, and one hour with your nose in the corner."

"Yeah, but ..."

"Hush." I turned back to the parrot. "Sorry, Birdie, we had a little departmental business to clean up." I cast a glance over to the iris patch and saw a pair of scheming little eyes peering out at us. "Okay, Pete, step out, I know you're there."

A moment later, the little creep oozed out into the light of day and began rubbing on the side of the house. "Well, well, it's Hankie the Wonderdog. How nice to see you again! We ought to go swimming some time, hee hee." He looked up at the parrot and batted his eyes. "My my, what a pretty bird."

I turned to Dink. "That's Pete, the local cat. He loves birds, but not for any reasons that should make you happy. He's not very smart, but if you get off that perch, he'll eat you. I'm sorry to put it that way, but you might as well ..." Now the bird was standing on one leg and pecking at his foot. "Hey, rookie, don't scratch your feet during my lecture!"

In a squawking voice, the bird said, "Polly want a cracker."

Drover was amazed. "Oh my gosh, he can talk!"

"He's a parrot, son. They don't actually talk. They repeat meaningless phrases."

"Yeah, but who's Polly?"

I stuck my nose in his face. "The parrot was babbling, and Polly is a meaningless nobody."

"Can I have a cracker, too?"

"No." I turned back to the bird. "Okay, pal, that's your orientation. You've met the staff of the Security Division and the local cat. I guess that's it. Nobody's glad you're here, so have a nice day. Or don't. We really don't care."

I whirled around and marched away. Behind me, I heard a squawking voice say, "Awk! Polly's a meaningless nobody! Polly's a meaningless nobody! Awk!"

That should have been my first clue that this bird was going to cause trouble, but I had other things on my mind. All at once, I ... uh, felt a strange craving for ... crackers.

CHAPTER FIVE

Loper's Present

We didn't have any crackers, but we had Co-op dog food, and I knew where to find it. Drover followed me up the hill to the machine shed. I went straight to the overturned Ford hubcap that served as our dog bowl.

I refuse to rave and rant about how insulting it is that our people feed the entire Security Division out of an old hubcap. They're too cheap to buy their dogs a decent food bowl, and that's really sad.

A lot of ranches serve their dogs fresh sirloin steak on a china plate. It makes a statement, see. It tells the world, "These dogs are special and we know it. They work around the clock, protecting our cattle, our equipment, our children, everything we own in this world, from dark and snicker forces, and by George, we're proud of them!"

Sinister forces, I guess it should be, not snicker forces.

Yes, that's the way your better grade of ranch dogs ought to be treated, with respect and maybe even a little bit of reverence, but I'm employed on a cheap outfit that . . .

Do you know where they got that hubcap? They didn't go to the Ford dealer in town and order a new one from the parts department. Oh no, that kind of extravagance might have thrown the entire ranch operation into bankrubble.

Loper found it on the side of the road, in the ditch!

I know I shouldn't let this bother me, and most of the time I take it with a grain of sand, but every once in a while, it just comes flooding out.

Sorry, it won't happen again.

Where were we? Oh yes, Dink the parrot. I had taken time out of my busy schedule to give him an introduction into life on our ranch. Did it do any good? It was hard to know. Before my presentation, he'd looked like a dumb bird. After I'd schooled him for half an hour, he didn't look any dumber, so maybe it did him some good.

Not that I cared. Educating birds isn't part of

my job. I'll give 'em a few tips now and then, but pulling the entire bird population up the Mountain of Knowledge isn't something you'll see me doing, or wanting to do.

Have we discussed my Position On Birds? Maybe so, but let's go over it again. As a whole, they are noisy, messy, and disrespectful of ranch property. Every summer, billions of them hang out in ranch trees, where they twitter and cheep and do their meaningless birdie things. They drive me nuts, but a dog can't spend his whole life barking at the little morons.

I met a pelican once and he turned out to be not such a bad guy. But ugly? Wow. The word "ugly" was invented the day pelicans showed up.

What was that guy's name? I don't remember, so maybe we weren't as good friends as I thought. Let's just skip it.

The point is, I have very little use for birds of any kind, but all at once, we had a parrot on the ranch. If he kept his mouth shut and minded his own business, he and I would get along okay. If he ran his beak and caused trouble, he would find no friends in the Security Division.

Anyway, Drover and I made our way up the hill to the machine shed, where we launched ourselves into the daily, dismal routine of trying to extract nourishment from the slop they leave in our dog bowl—which, you already know, wasn't a bowl at all, but a rusted, stinking Ford hubcap.

It contained a substance called Co-op Dog Food. They sell it at the feed store and it comes in a fifty-pound bag. It's made out of all the stuff that you can't feed to cows, hogs, goldfish, or pet canaries. They dump it into a big vat, add some sawdust and grease, and bag it up.

No human would eat the stuff, but they feed it to their dogs and feel no shame at all. I mean, when we look up from the bowl and give 'em the expression that says, "Is this all?" it makes 'em mad, and they start muttering about "ungrateful dogs."

Oh well. Food is only food, but here's a piece of inside information: Dogs who are fed Co-op dog food find it very hard to keep a professional attitude about chickens. I'll *slurp* say no more.

So Drover and I crunched our way through our pitiful ration of dry, tasteless dog food kernels. The day had warmed up by then, so we, uh, held a meeting of the Executive Committee in the shade of the machine shed. There, we kemped a clerse eye on snicklefritz snerk snobly porkchops ... kept a close eye on events down in the yard, shall we say, and perhaps I dozed off a time or two.

Yes, I'm sure I did. The morning spent with

Drover and Dink the parrot had pretty muchly worn me down to a nubbin, and don't forget that unfortunate episode with the cat. I needed some rest to restore my precious bodily fluids, and I'm not ashamed to admit it.

I needed sleep, so I slept. I awoke sometime in the late afternoon, when Data Control sent out an All Points Bulletin (APB). I was sitting in the Ready Room when the announcement blared over the speakers: "Attention! We are tracking an unidentified vehicle on radar, incoming. Launch all dogs! Repeat: launch all dogs!"

I grabbed my gear, dashed outside, and dived into the cockpit of my XM-235, whose rocket engines were already humming. (Our ground crew does a great job.) Moments later, I was streaking through the cloudless afternoon sky, in hot pursuit of . . .

Okay, it was Loper, back from his trip to town. Ha ha. No big deal, just a routine interception procedure. This happens two or three times every day. A lot of mutts don't trouble themselves to do those Scrambles in the heat of the day (Drover, for instance; he was a no-show), but I respond to every alert.

You never know who might be in the next car

or pickup that turns at the mailbox and comes creeping down the road toward the house. Today, it was Loper. Tomorrow, it might be a burglar, an enemy spy, or some kind of alien space monster, disguised as a postal employee.

They are clever beyond our wildest dreams, and we must remain alert.

I barked Loper a greeting and gave him an escort all the way to the house. By the time his feet hit the ground, I had splashed Secret Encoding Fluid on both tires on the right side of his pickup. I was on my way to the left rear tire when he reached the yard gate.

And I heard him say, "What in the world? Slim! Come here!"

I canceled the Encoding Procedure and headed for the gate, just as Slim came sludging around the southwest corner of the house, moving at his usual pace: slow.

Loper's arm and finger shot out and pointed. "What is that?"

"It's a parrot."

"I see it's a parrot. What's he doing on my back porch?"

Slim arrived at the gate, removed his hat, and wiped the sweat away from his face. "Well, it don't look like he's doing much of anything, just sitting there."

Loper wasn't amused. "Where did he come from? Who did this to me?"

"Well, Deputy Kile happened by."

"He *happened* by? And he happened to have a parrot in his car? And he happened to think that I needed one? Is that your story?"

Slim shrugged. "Well, that's pretty much what happened, all right. I tried to tell him you wouldn't be interested in paying a thousand bucks for an exotic, high-powered talking bird."

"Well, you got that right."

"So he left it as a gift—for Father's Day, I think it was."

Loper was fuming. He glared at his feet, then glared at the sky. "Somebody needs killing. I don't know if it's you or Bobby Kile, or both of you. That bird *goes*!" He stormed over to the perch, threw his hands in the air, and yelled, "Hyah! Get out of here!" Old Dink just sat there, didn't even flinch. That made Loper madder than ever, and he whirled back to Slim. "Can't he fly? What's wrong with him?"

Slim's shoulders rose and fell. "I don't know. Maybe ya'll have bonded and he don't want to leave."

Loper stomped back to the gate and aimed a finger at Slim. "The bird goes. I'll put up with cattle, horses, cats, dogs, two children, and a conniving hired hand, but no birds."

"Loper, he can talk."

Loper's eyes almost bugged out of his head. "So can you! I don't want to adopt either one of you. Get that bird..."

He didn't finish his sentence, because just then, Sally May's car pulled up into the driveway behind the house. We'd all been so occupied with Loper's screeching, nobody had heard her coming.

The instant she stepped out of the car, her eyes were on that parrot. She was smiling and she said, "What a beautiful bird!"

I happened to be looking at Loper at that moment, and a terrible expression appeared on his face. "Hon, there's been a mistake..."

Too late. She swept through the yard gate and went straight to the perch and began admiring Dink. She turned back to Loper and said, "You know, I've always wanted a parrot."

Loper was mouse-trapped and he knew it. He turned back to Slim and ... boys, you talk about Killer Eyes! He hissed, "You'll pay for this. I don't know how or when, but you'll pay."

By that time, Slim's grin had escaped the teeth that were trying to hold it down. "Heh. Loper, you're trying to hang the wrong man. Hee. I was just an innocent bystander."

"Paybacks are terrible, Slim!"

With that, Loper left our little gathering and stormed into the house, and the parrot started talking. "Hyah, get out of here! What's wrong with him? Can't he fly?"

Sally May was shocked and delighted. She looked at Slim. "My stars, that sounded just like Loper's voice. Does the bird have a name?"

"Dink."

"Dink? What kind of name is that?" She turned an admiring gaze on the bird. "But him's a beautiful bird, isn't him? Yes him is. And him can talk so well!"

When lady of the house starts speaking baby-talk to a parrot, it means that the bird is in like Flynn—and fixing to get promoted from a yard bird to a house bird.

He did. Sally May was so impressed with Dink, she moved his perch into the kitchen, so he could keep her company while she started supper.

CHAPTER SIX

A Voice
in the Night

Slim was still wearing that naughty little grin. He winked at me and said, "Ain't it nice when you can match up a lady with the parrot of her dreams? Heh. That'll teach Loper to stick me with the yard work."

He went back to his mowing, a happy man.

I stayed at the yard gate and monitored the events inside the house. Something told me that this situation needed watching.

Through the open window, I could hear Dink putting on a show. "Awk! Polly want a cracker. Pieces of eight, pieces of eight! Pretty bird, pretty bird. Sheriff's Department, Deputy Kile speaking. Paybacks are terrible. Awk!"

Yes sir, he put on quite a show, and it lasted exactly thirty-two minutes. That's how long it took Dink to wear out his welcome. The back door burst open and out stepped Loper, carrying the star of the show.

Loper planted the perch on the perch... the porch on the perch... he planted the perch on the porch (that's hard to say, isn't it, ha) and he roasted the bird with his eyes. "Bird, keep up that racket and you might end up in my deep freeze."

Loper stomped back into the house, slamming the door behind him. Dink sat there on his perch, blinking his weird eyes and scratching his feathers with his beak. Then, in a wonderful imitation of Sally May's voice, he squawked, "Pieces of eight! Pretty bird in the deep freeze!"

I couldn't resist putting in my two cents. "Hey Dink, it didn't take you long to get canned, did it? Ha. In a quiet moment, you might try to remember what I told you: Keep your trap shut. Nobody on this ranch needs a blabbermouth bird."

With that stinging rebuke, I whirled around and marched away. I hadn't gone more than ten steps when I heard what sounded like my own voice, saying, "Nobody needs a blabbermouth bird!"

I had to admit it was pretty amazing, what that bird could do. On the other hand, we have to remember that mere imitation is a minor talent. Anyone can do it.

Hmm. Okay, I couldn't do it and neither could any other dog I knew, but imitation is still a minor talent. It's pure mimicry. No parrot will ever achieve greatness, because all they can do is repeat someone else's words.

See, your truly gifted individuals create from scratch, pulling words and graceful sentences out of the shrouded vapors of the fog of the imagination. That was a pretty awesome sentence right there, wasn't it? I'm not one to honk my own whistle, but when I put my mind to composition, the parrots might as well pack their bags and go back to Punkin' Center ... or wherever they come from.

Where do they come from? Someplace with jungles and zoos, where noisy birds sit around in trees, chattering imitations of other noisy birds sitting around in trees.

But the point is that your average garden-variety parrot has a tiny skill that can entertain an audience for about thirty-two minutes, whereas your higher breeds of cowdog can write poems and songs. Dogs improve over time, don't you see, as we become older, deeper, and wiser. Parrots merely grow tiresome.

I could go on, but that's all the time we have to spend on parrots. Hey, I had a ranch to run, and before darkness fell, I had to do my Evening Walk-Around, checking out the corrals, the calf shed, Emerald Pond, the saddle house, and the chicken house *slurp*.

Hold it! Please disregard the "slurp" at the end of that sentence. It meant nothing, almost nothing at all, and some readers might get the wrong impression. Let's face it, some dogs go around all day, dreaming of the moment when they can bump off a careless *slurp* ...

Let's just say that I was misquoted, and move along.

I did my evening patrol, and darkness fell exactly where it always falls, right on top of the ranch, and everything got dark. Around ten o'clock, after I had put in my usual eighteen-hour day, I strolled into the lobby of the Security Division's Vast Office Complex and rode the elevator up to the twelfth floor.

When I strolled into the office, Drover was already there, curled up in a ball. He raised up and said, "Oh hi. How's the parrot?"

"The parrot is fine."

"I never thought we'd have a parrot on the ranch, did you?"

"No." I checked messages and stared at the stack of reports on my desk. I was too worn out to read them. I flopped down on my gunnysack bed and surrendered myself to its warm embrace.

After a few moments of peace and quiet, Drover said, "Aren't you going to say good night?"

"No."

"How come?"

"Because the only way this will be a good night is if you let me go to sleep."

"Yeah, but then you can't say good night."

I raised my head and gave him a glare. "Drover, what is your problem?"

"Well, it kind of hurts my feelings that you won't tell me good night."

"All right, good night!" I lay back down and prepared for sleep.

"You know what? That rhymes." I tried to ignore him. "You said, 'All right, good night.' It's a neat rhyme. I love rhymes, don't you?"

"No."

"So do I. They're kind of like flowers. They make the world a little more prettiful."

"Prettiful is not a word."

"I was just checking to see if you were awake."

"I'm not."

"What would you think if I sang you a little song?"

"Please go away."

"I wrote it myself and I think it's pretty neat. Ready? Here goes." And believe it or not, the little mutt burst into song. Check this out.

There Once Was a Doggie

There once was a doggie named Noodle.
His mom was a Frenchified poodle.
His dad was a grench
Who didn't speak French
And often was in a bad moodle.

There once was a doggie name Buzzy.
His muzzle was narrow and fuzzy.
He tripped on his ear
And fell on his rear.
He wasn't intelligent, was he?

There once was a doggie name Rocket.
He kept a pet bone in his pocket.
But times got so bad,
He got hungry and had
To take it to Dallas and hock it.

There once was a doggie named Nettie.
She ate a whole can of spaghetti.
But then she threw up
And stared at the stuff
And thought she had swallowed confetti.

I tried to sleep through his song, but it turned out to be so bad, I found myself listening to it, just to see if it could get any worse. It did.

I heaved a sigh and sat up. "All right, that's all I can stand. Enough."

He was grinning, so proud of himself he could hardly sit still. "What do you think? Tell me the truth."

"Drover, that is sick. In the first place, throwing up is hardly a proper subject for a song. What if the little children heard it? Do you want to encourage the children to go around throwing up all the time?"

"I never thought of that."

"In the second place, there is no such thing as a 'bad moodle.'"

"Yeah, but it rhymed."

"It rhymed, but it was a cheating rhyme."

"Yeah, but sometimes I have to cheat to get my rhymes to work."

"Yes, and look what it's done to you. You've

produced a song that not only encourages children to throw up, but also teaches them to cheat. What kind of world do you want these kids to live in?"

He rolled his eyes around. "Well, I was bored and wanted to sing."

"Bored! I'm worn to a frazzle, and you're bored?"

"Yeah, I slept most of the day."

"Oh brother!" I leaped to my feet, scratched up my gunnysack, circled it three times, and collapsed. "I'm going to sleep. If you want to jabber all night, go right ahead."

"Really? Oh good. Let's see, what can I talk about?"

"On second thought, hush."

"Oh drat." There was a moment of silence, then, "Hey, did you notice that 'drat' almost rhymes with 'trap'? I wonder if that means anything."

"Yes, it means hush your mouth and go to sleep!"

Whew. At last, I managed to shut off his noise and began driveling off into a purseful sneep . . . honking sassafras vanilla swamp rat . . . zzzzzzzzzzzzzzzzzzzzzzzzzzz.

Perhaps I finally managed to doze off. Yes, I'm sure I did, and it was wonderful sleep, exactly what my poor body needed after an exhausting day of running the ranch. But then . . .

At first, I thought I'd heard a voice. It said, and this is a direct quote, it said, "Hank, get over here and bark at the moon!"

Data Control wasn't functioning too well at that hour of the night, but I managed to get a Confirm/No Confirm. The message from DC said, "False alarm. You're dreaming. Go back to sleep."

Great. That was exactly what I wanted to...

"Hank, get over here and bark at the moon!"

I shot straight up in bed. Not only had I heard the voice again, but this time I even recognized to whom it belonged: Loper. I noticed that Drover was awake too—awake, sitting up, and listening with perked ears.

I whispered, "Did you hear that?"

"Yeah, and it sounded like Loper. But why would he want you to bark at the moon?"

"I have no idea. It seems crazy, doesn't it?"

"Yeah, 'cause every time we bark at the moon, he tells us to be quiet."

"Exactly. Maybe we both had the same dream at the same time. I mean, that happens sometimes, right?"

"I'll bet that was it. Let's go back to sleep."

"Roger that. Good night."

I stretched out on my wonderful gunnysack and began drifting away on a cloud of...

"Hank, get over here and bark at the moon!"

I flew out of my gunnysack and hit the ground with all four feet. "Drover, that wasn't a dream. We've been called into action. Boots on the ground, soldier, let's move out!"

And with that, we went streaking through the darkness to begin a mission that would take us to ... we had no idea what this was all about, but in Security Work, we answer the call and work out the details when we can.

CHAPTER SEVEN

We Bark at
the Moon

It was a short flight down to the yard gate, but
I used every second of the trip to work through
the details of this case. There were exactly ten details. You want to take a peek at my notes? Okay,
I guess we have time.

Detail Number One: Loper, the owner of the
ranch, had gotten out of bed, gone to the back door,
and yelled out an order to the Security Division.

Detail Number Two: Yelling orders at night
was something he rarely did, because ... well, because he usually sleeps at night.

Detail Number Three: Odder still, he had
given us a direct order to *bark at the moon*.

Detail Number Four: This was an order he
had never given us before. Never.

Detail Number Seven: Even so, the entire staff of the Security Division had heard the order, loud and clear, delivered three times in a row.

Detail Number Ten: There was, in fact, a bright half-moon hanging in the sky, right above the roof of the house.

If we'd had only three or four details on this case, we might have written them off as a coincidence, but you know what they say about ten details. "Ten details are ten times detailer than one." So there you are. We had ourselves a major case. We just didn't know where it would take us.

We arrived at the yard gate at approximately 0100. In other words, it was past midnight. We crept up to the gate on silent paws. There, I halted the column and did a visual scan of the entire house and yard.

The scan revealed ... well, not much. I saw a dark house, a couple of trees in silhouette against the moonlit sky, and a sleeping parrot on his perch on the porch. Oh yes, and a bright half-moon suspended in the air above the peak of the roof.

I turned to Drover and whispered, "I don't see anything unusual, do you?"

"Well, it's kind of dark."

"Exactly, but it gets that way at night."

"Yeah, but what if there's a monster out there?"

"We'll just have to take our chances." I took a deep breath of air. "Okay, men, our orders are simple and clear. We'll do a countdown and bark at the moon."

"That moon up there?"

"That's correct. Aim your barks at the very center of the moon. That way, if your aim's off by a few centipedes, you'll still hit something solid. Ready? Assume your Barking Position." We spread all four legs and found comfortable firing positions. "Set muzzle elevation at 47 degrees. Open outer doors. Arm the weapon. Stand by. We are in the countdown: three, two, one ... fire away!"

Boy, you should have been there to hear us. It was an amazing barrage of barking, blast after blast of huge barks that came from downtown and went all the way up to the moon. Fellers, I wouldn't have wanted to be the moon on that particular night, because the boys from the Security Division were putting on a show.

For five solid minutes, we fired off round after round, blast upon blast, until at last I had to give the command to cease firing. I mean, if you don't give those muzzles a chance to cool down, they'll melt like ...

Did you hear that? It was a man's voice and it seemed to be coming from inside the house. In fact, our instruments gave us a more precise location. The voice seemed to be coming from somewhere near Loper and Sally May's bedroom.

Drover heard it too. "Gosh, that sounded like Loper."

"Indeed it did, but why would he telling us to be quiet? We're just following his orders."

In the silence of the night, we pondered this puzzling turn of events. Then Drover said, "Wait, I've got it. He didn't say, 'Be quiet.' He said, 'Knock it off.'"

"Yes? So what's your point?"

"He doesn't want us to be quiet, he wants us to *knock off* the moon."

I gave that some thought. "Of course! Don't you get it? He wants us to bark louder and blast that moon right out of the sky."

"Yeah, but I'm not sure I can bark any louder."

"I know, me either, but we have to give it our best shot. Failure is not an option for this Security Division. Okay, prepare the weapons for Sequence Two. Reload, take ten deep breaths, and realign muzzles." We moved back into our firing positions. "Restart clock and resume countdown. We are in the countdown: three, two, one. Fire!"

I didn't think we had enough juice to bark any louder, but somehow we did it. Boy, you talk about blasting the moon! We could see sparks and chunks of green cheese flying off the surface. We were well on the way to knocking it completely out of the sky, when ...

"*Meatheads! Shut up that barking!*"

Huh?

I gave the signal to cease firing. Our guns fell silent. For a long moment, neither of us could speak. I mean, this was very confusing. Then Drover said, "He called us meatheads."

"Do you think he was yelling at *us*?"

"Well, we were the only ones barking."

"Good point."

The little mutt looked so discouraged, I thought he might start crying. "It really hurts my feelings. I tried so hard! And it stirred ub by sidusses."

I laid a paw on his shoulder. "You did a great job, son. I've never seen you do a better job of barking." I glanced around and heaved a sigh. "Well, let's pack our gear and return to base."

We formed a line and began the march back to our sleeping quarters beneath the gas tanks. We hadn't gone more than twenty yards, when Loper screeched at us again. "*Meatheads! Get up here and bark at the moon!*"

Drover and I stopped in our tracks and exchanged glances. I said, "What's going on here? He called us meatheads for barking, now he's calling us meatheads for not barking."

"Yeah, and we're not even meatheads."

"You're exactly right. Who does he think he's talking to, a bunch of stray cats?"

"Yeah, we don't have to take that."

There was a moment of silence. "Actually, Drover, we do. We're the elite troops of the Security Division. We have to follow orders, even when they don't make sense. Come on, let's hit it another lick."

Even though we were exhausted from this ordeal (the recoil from those heavy barks will wear you down), we trudged back to the yard gate. But before we could resume our firing positions, I noticed that we had company.

A cat. Pete.

He was sitting inside the yard, on the other side of the fence, wearing his usual insolent smirk and purring like a little ... I don't know what. Motorboat. Refrigerator. "Hankie, you seem to be having some trouble."

"I don't know what you're talking about."

"Well ..." He grinned and fluttered his eyelids. "It's the middle of the night, and everyone is screaming at you."

"Not everyone, Pete, just Loper."

"But still, it seems odd, doesn't it? I wonder if there's more here than meets the eye."

I noticed that the lips around my teeth had begun to twitch. I had to struggle to control my savage instincts. "What are you saying, Kitty? And hurry up. We have work to do."

He lifted his left paw and began licking it with long strokes of his tongue. "Hankie, I've been here all night, watching the whole fiasco from start to finish."

"I know nothing about a fiasco."

"That's the point, Hankie." He stopped licking his paw and stared at me with his yellow cattish eyes. "I don't know why I'm telling you this, Hankie, but you've been set up."

"No, you got it backward which, I might point out, is typical cat logic. We haven't been *set up*, Pete, we've been *upset*. We're upset because we're getting conflicting orders from the same man."

"Well, that's what you think, Hankie. Actually, it's a lot more interesting than that. I might give you some helpful advice . . . if you'll ask nicely."

All at once, I couldn't hold back a rush of laughter. "Ha ha ha. Helpful advice? From you? Hey Pete, correct me if I'm wrong, but aren't you the same guy who tried to tear off my ears this morning?"

He shrugged. "Don't stand around and watch when a cat's about to be pitched into a stock tank. We cause collateral damage."

"Yeah, well, here's a news flash. Number one, I never take advice from cats. Number two, if I ever did, I wouldn't ask nicely for it. Number three, if you keep standing there, running your mouth, I'll give you a few lessons on collateral damage."

Drover let out a giggle. "Hee hee. Good shot, Hank! You really got him on that one."

"And number four, go chase your tail. We have work to do." I whirled away from the cat and spoke to Drover. "Assume firing positions."

Pete shrugged. "You'll be sorry, Hankie, but I'll enjoy the show."

"You do that, Kitty, and when the moon comes crashing down, I hope it lands right on top of your head." Imagine the cat trying to give me advice. Ha! What a joke. "Elevate muzzles. Open outer doors. We're into the countdown sequence: three, two, one. Blast away!"

You'll be proud to know that I aimed my first three barks at Pete's face and gave him Train Horns. Hee hee. You should have seen him. It was hilarious. The little creep never saw it coming. I blew him out of his tracks and sent him back to the iris patch.

"Hiss, reeeeer!"

The finest music in this world is the sound of an unhappy cat. I love it!

But I didn't have time to enjoy the music. I had to get back to work, firing those huge 250-mm barks. Drover and I found a rhythm and, fellers, we were pumping them out like . . .

Huh? That was odd. The back door opened and someone came out. I gave Drover the signal to cease firing, and we studied the figure that had come out on the porch. It appeared to be an adult male. I sensed that he was "adult" because he was bigger than a child, don't you see, and "male" because he wore boxer shorts and cowboy boots—a pretty strange combination that only a man would wear.

His hair was . . . well, a mess, what else can you say? Some of it hung down over his eyes, some of it stuck up in the back, and several sprigs stuck out on the side. Like I said, it was a mess.

He stepped off the porch and came down the sidewalk toward us. I narrowed my eyes and took a closer look . . . and suddenly realized that I HAD NEVER SEEN THIS MAN BEFORE!

CHAPTER EIGHT

A Victory for Science

Boy, you talk about something that will send a shock all the way out to the end of your tail! That'll do it, seeing a complete stranger walk out of a house that was supposed to be occupied by Loper and Sally May. In the middle of the night.

Who was that guy and what kind of crinimal mischief was he up to?

For a moment, I was frozen by ... I might as well go ahead and say it. I was frozen by fear—pure, unambiguous fear, the kind of raw emotion that makes a dog want to drop everything and head for tall timber.

No ordinary dog could have resisted the urge to flee, but somehow I did. How? Training and discipline had a lot to do with it. Also, paralyzing fear tends to make your legs useless for a retreat. Bottom line: my legs were too scared to move, so the rest of me had to remain on the job.

At last I was able to speak in a shaky whisper. "Drover, I don't want to alarm you, but a stranger just walked out of the house. And there's more bad news. I don't think I can run. My legs just quit on me." I happened to be looking at him and saw a goofy smile form upon his mouth. "Drover, let me repeat: I think I'm disabled, but you're grinning."

"Yeah, 'cause he's not a stranger."

"I beg your pardon? Come back on that."

"It's Loper. Who else would come out of Loper's house in the middle of the night?"

"Don't get smart with me, you little squeakbox! I'm telling you, that man is not . . ."

Huh?

Okay, we can relax. Ha ha. It was Loper. I mean, who else would you expect to walk out of Loper's house in the middle of the night? Ha ha.

But, seriously, sometimes the stress of this job will get you down. After you've worked an eighteen-hour shift and they call you back out on another case, your mind starts playing tricks on you. No kidding.

So, yes, it was Loper, the owner of our ranch,

coming down the sidewalk toward us, and carrying ... what was that thing? A plastic pitcher? Yes, he was carrying a plastic pitcher, and anyone could have mistaken him for a total stranger. I mean, he was half-naked in his boxer shorts and his hair looked like a packrat's nest.

Hey, in the dark of night, we get faulty information and sometimes we make bad calls. It could have happened to any dog.

Well, I felt a huge sense of relief. Since he wasn't screeching at us, I had every reason to suppose that he had taken notice of our work and had come out to ... I don't know, bring us fresh water or maybe some lemonade.

At lot of ranchers will do that for their dogs, bring 'em a pitcher of lemonade when they've been putting in a long, hard night. Studies show that long periods of heavy barking will inflame the tissues around the vocational cords, don't you know, and nothing will soothe inflamed throatalary tissues better than lemonade.

He walked up to the gate and looked down at us. I switched all circuits over to Humble and Proud, thumped my tail on the ground, and gave him a big cowdog smile. I was so intent on my presentation of Humble and Proud, I hardly noticed that Drover had vanished. I mean, poof, gone.

Loper spoke. "Well, I guess you're having a grand old time out here, huh?"

A grand old time? Well, I wouldn't have put it exactly that way, but we'd certainly stayed busy, trying to fulfill our mission.

"What part of 'stop barking' don't you dogs understand?"

Uh . . . I didn't know how to respond to that. See, we'd been getting these confusing messages . . .

"Do you need a hearing aid?"

Oh no, thanks. My ears were fine.

"Well, I brought you one."

Huh?

What a cheap trick! You know what he did? He poured a pitcher of cold water right on top of my head! And then he screeched, "Now shut up your barking and let me get some sleep! Next time, I'll bring the shotgun."

And with that, he stomped back into the house and slammed the door behind him. The slamming of the door woke up Dink the parrot and he squawked, "Poor doggie, pieces of eight, Polly want a shotgun!"

I stared at the bird and found myself wondering . . . nah, he was just a dumb bird.

I whirled around and marched back to the office—dripping water, I might add—and found

my assistant cowering under his gunnysack bed. He heard me come in and peeked out from under his sack.

"Oh, hi. How'd it go?"

"You left the field of battle, is how it went, and this will go into your record."

"Hank, I just figured it out."

"He dumped a pitcher of water on top of my head."

"It was the parrot."

"I've never been so outraged!"

"He's a troublemaker."

"What does it take to please these people?"

"That's what Pete was trying to tell you."

"And then he had the nerve to call it a hearing aid!"

"You need one."

"Well, by George, the next time Loper wants someone to bark at the moon, he can do it himself."

"Hank?"

Had I heard a voice? I narrowed my eyes and ... oh yes, Drover was there beside me. "What?"

"It was the parrot. He's the one who told us to bark at the moon."

"What?" I stared at the runt for a whole minute. "Did you just say ... you think ..." All at once,

I went into a fit of laughing. I couldn't control myself. I mean, Drover had said some crazy things in his life, but this might have been the nuttiest.

I laughed for a solid minute, and we're talking about laughing so hard, I couldn't even grab a breath of air. When I finally managed to get control of things, I ordered the little mutt to come out from under his bed. I made him sit down, while I stood in front of him and gave him a lecture.

"Drover, I've told you this before, but let's go over it one more time. Dink is a parrot, a bird. Parrots have a tiny skill for repeating words and phrases, but they don't talk. They mimic."

"I think this one can talk. He's a troublemaker. That's why the deputy wanted to get rid of him."

I spent a long moment weighing both sides of the argument. At last, I came up with a plan. "All right, Drover, let's settle this by using the scientific method."

"Gosh, that's a good idea."

"Yes. Instead of carrying on a pointless argument, we're going to call upon science to settle it once and for all."

"Oh goodie. We're going to test your theory?"

"Not exactly." I gave him a withering glare. "We're going to stick your nose in the corner and let you stand there until you understand that parrots don't talk."

His jaw dropped in surprise. "That's not science!"

"Of course it is. Science already knows that parrots don't talk, so testing would be a tee-total waste of time."

"Yeah, but . . ."

"The question science must resolve is, how long will it take you to admit what science figured out hundreds of years ago?"

"Are you serious?"

I showed him two rows of gleaming fangs. "Do I look serious? To the corner, move it!"

He whined and moaned, but I didn't care. Even though my body was crying out for sleep, I stood right there and watched, just to make sure he didn't cheat. You don't think Drover would cheat? Ha. Listen, he'd spent so much time around the local cat, he couldn't be trusted, even with a simple scientific experiment.

Fifteen minutes later, I was dying of boredom. "Okay, time's up. Put your pencils down and close your test booklets."

"I don't have a pencil."

"Don't argue with me. Have you come up with the correct answer?"

"Parrots can't talk."

"Excellent. Parrots can't talk, they can only ... what?"

"Mimic."

"Congratulations, son, you've passed the test. You see what can happen when you apply yourself and do your homework?"

"It's all baloney."

"I beg your pardon?"

"I said, I wish I had a baloney sandwich."

"Yes, and your wishing is like fishing. All it takes is a good bite. Ha ha." I waited for him to laugh. He didn't. "That was a joke. Wishing, fishing, bait, bite, sandwich ..."

"I don't get it."

I took a deep breath. "Okay, it's obvious that you need to spend a little more time with your nose in the corner."

"Oh, I get it now. Fishing, wishing. Hee hee hee. Great joke!"

"Do you really mean that?"

"Oh yeah, it's the great jokest I ever heard."

"Very well, you may remove your nose from the corner. Let's try to grab some sleep."

He gave a yip of triumph and scampered over to his gunnysack. I fluffed up my sack ... boy, that thing was beginning to stink, but what do you expect when the owner of the ranch is too cheap to buy fresh bedding for the staff? We do the best with what we have.

When I hit the sack, I was already sailing my little boat across the Sleepful Sea, but then I heard a muttering voice. It said, "Parrots talk."

I sat straight up and looked around. I saw no one except Drover, who was occupying the bunk next to mine. "Did you say something?"

"Who me? Nope, not a word."

"That's odd. I thought I heard someone muttering about parrots."

"Oh, that. Yeah, it was me."

"Aha! Drover, is it possible that, after all we've been through, you said, 'Parrots talk'?"

"No, I said, 'Parents talk,' but it sounded like 'parrots,' 'cause by dose is stobbed ub again."

"Oh, well that explains it. Good night."

"Nighty night." There was a moment of peaceful silence, then I heard his voice again. "Parrots really do talk."

I sat up in bed. "Of course they do. That's how they communicate with their children. And by the way, you need to get your nose fixed. It's starting to annoy me. Now, for the last time, good night."

I melted into the warm folds of my beloved gunnysack and surrendered my grip on the world. I'd put in a long, hard day, dealing with screeching cats, squawking birds, and Drover's little outburst anti-scientific rebellion.

But, you know, when you stay the course and stork with your prissibles, every snork seems to donkey the turnip greens ... *zzzzzzzzzzzzzzzzzzzz zzzzzzzzzzzzzzzz*.

CHAPTER NINE

Sally May and I Patch Things Up

Perhaps I dozed off. Yes, I'm sure I did, and the next thing I knew, it was daily broadlight, and we're talking about half the day gone. Good grief, I'd slept past noon!

I leaped out of bed, planted all four feet upon the earth, and tried to get my bearings. They seemed to be rolling around inside my head, which didn't come as a total surprise. I mean, I'd been up half the night, doing counseling with Drover, and that will cause the marbles and bearings to roll around inside your head.

Sometimes I worry about the little mutt. I really do. When one of your employees comes out and declares that he doesn't believe in science, what can you say? It's a cause for concern.

Speaking of Drover, he was still curled up in a little ball, honking and muttering in his sleep, so I left him there and hurried down to the house. To be honest, I was embarrassed that I'd stayed in bed so long.

You know me. I like to have my ranch in top shape before the people get out of bed. A lot of mutts don't care. They'll lollygag around and spend so much time in bed, they sprout roots. Not me. The Head of Ranch Security starts his day before daylight ... only I'd sort of flunked that one, but you should remember the reason. Drover.

By the time I reached the yard gate, I could see that the ranch was hopping with activity, and I remembered why. The church choir was coming out for a picnic and Sally May had every able-bodied citizen of our ranch community employed in some kind of meaningful activity.

Slim was trimming the cedar shrubs in front of the house. Loper was down at the picnic grounds, arranging tables and wiping them with a wet cloth. Little Alfred was picking up twigs and limbs— oh, and chasing grasshoppers. Heh. He probably thought nobody was watching, but I saw it.

He was goofing off. Your higher breeds of dogs don't miss much.

Dink the parrot was perched on his perch on

the porch, shuffling from one end of the perch to the other. Maybe he was pacing. I didn't know and I didn't care. What birds do is of no interest to me.

On the other hand, I couldn't help noticing that, for a bird, he was kind of handsome—if you could get past the fact that his nose made up two-thirds of his face. We're talking about a huge curved beak that left only a small space for the eyes or anything else. Oh, and he had no ears.

On impulse, I decided to be sociable. "Hey Dink, question. Was your mother's nose as big as yours? See, if a dog had such a nose, he would spend a lot of time alone. He would cry himself to sleep at night. He would have no girlfriends. You have pretty feathers, but the nose looks like a joke that got out of hand."

He looked at me and cocked his head to the side. "Pretty bird, pretty nose, awk."

"Well, you can say that if you want, pal, but saying it doesn't make it true. From where I sit, the only thing more ridiculous than a parrot's face would be the faces of two parrots."

"Polly want a cracker, Polly want a shotgun."

"Oh, and another thing. Your conversation is really boring."

"Awk! Pieces of eight, Sheriff's Department."

There, you see? Parrots *can't talk*. They just

repeat meaningless phrases. Why anyone would want to keep a parrot around, I couldn't understand. They make noise, they make a mess, they have no personality.

At that very moment, Sally May came out the back door. She wore faded blue jeans and a floppy work shirt, and a big straw hat on her ... well, on her head, of course. Where else would you find a straw hat?

Like I said, we don't miss much.

She was also carrying a cardboard box that contained ... something green and leafy, perhaps flowers. Yes, they were potted flowers, and I even knew their name: bazoonias.

She wore a pleasant expression on her face, and that brought a rush of joy to my heart. See, my relationship with Sally May had ... uh ... over the years, we'd shared a few precious moments, but also quite a few that hadn't been so precious.

Let's be frank. Sometimes I got the feeling that she didn't particularly like me. This had caused me more pain than you can imagine, because ... well, she was the Lady of the House, the wife of the ranch owner, and as Head of Ranch Security, I really needed to figure out how to get along with her. Pleasing her was an important part of my job.

In quiet moments, I often wondered how our

relationship had taken such a bad turn, and now and then I found myself thinking, "Maybe it's partly my fault." See, in the midst of our very stormiest periods, certain themes had come up over and over.

She wasn't fond of my smell.

She didn't appreciate me beating up her stupid ... uh, she felt that I needed to be kinder to her cat.

She had powerful objections to my digging holes in her garden and licking her on the ankles.

And, most poisonous of all, she seemed absolutely convinced that I had some kind of crazy desire to eat her chickens.

Slurp. Excuse me.

Well, you can imagine how deeply I was wounded by all these rumors and suspicions. It just broke my heart. After I had tried so hard to please her ... but you know what? The real test of a dog is how he responds to hard times. Any dog can look good when things are perfect, but when the going gets tough, can he rise above all the pettiness and make something of his relationships with the people in his life?

That's the real question, fellers, and it separates the sheep from the goats. Loyal dogs don't quit, even when our hearts are broken. We keep coming back until we figure out how to work through our problems.

Hencely, even though I was tempted to tuck my tail and slink away when she walked back into my life, I stood my ground. I went to Slow Sincere Wags on the tail section and beamed her a look that said, "Sally May, we can't repair past mistakes, but I have a feeling that this is the day we're going to patch things up."

Hmm. She didn't see me. A lot of dogs would have gotten discouraged and quit right there. Not me. I barked.

Oops. Maybe that was the wrong thing to do. Her head snapped around and her eyes ... yipes. You know, she's a wonderful lady, but she's got this wrinkle line between her eyebrows, and when it appears ... gulp ... it's hard to stand your ground.

She spoke. "You barked all night long."

Uh, yes, and her husband had spoken to me about that.

"Why do you do that?"

Well, we'd ... we'd been ordered to shoot down the moon. No kidding. In the light of day, that sounded kind of silly, but that's what we'd been told to do.

She shook her head. "You're hopeless." She went over to the flowerbed beside the house, dropped down on her hands and knees, and began spading up the ground with a hand trowel.

I'm sure she didn't intend for her words to puncture my heart. I'm sure she didn't see the tears that flooded my eyes. She had no idea how deeply those three words ... two words ... infected me. See, if you're a loyal dog, the two words that can bring you crashing to the ground are: *"You're hopeless."*

You know why? Because it means, "There's no reason to hope for something better. This is the end. We're finished. I'm walking away from this relationship."

Suddenly, I found myself staring at a wasted life, years of trying to please her and trying to bring a little smile to her lips ... and it all came crashing down like rafters in a burning house. And, fellers, I just fell apart.

I'm not a dog who shows his emotions very often. That kind of dog doesn't last long in the Security Business. But her words struck me like an ocean wave and swept me out into a sea of emotion. I started crying, moaning. I couldn't help it.

If I'd had a crafty, calculating mind, I might

have planned all this, knowing that she found it hard to ignore the sobs and cries of a dog whose heart had been shattered. But it wasn't planned, none of it. It was totally spondifferous.

Spongilational.

Spontutational.

What is the word? Of all the times to draw a blank ... wait, here we go. SPONTANEOUS. My emotional so-forth was totally spontaneous. There was nothing planned or crafty about it. Her words had pierced my heart like an arrow, and I broke down in tears and weeping.

I moaned. I didn't care who heard it. Nothing mattered anymore.

Through the blur of tears, I saw her head come up from the flowerbed. She turned and looked at me. Remember that wrinkle line in her forehead, the one that tells dogs and little boys that they had better run? Well, it was still there, like a symbol chiseled onto a tombstone, but unless my eyes were playing tricks, it was beginning to melt.

No kidding. She heaved a weary sigh and rose to her feet. She dusted the grass off the knees of her jeans and looked up at the sky. She shook her head and looked at me. "Hank, please don't moan. You make me feel like a mean old hag."

Really? Hmm. We could build on that. I, uh, turned up the volume and leaned into another outburst of moaning.

She came to the gate and stood over me. I could see several emotions on her face, some of them hopeful and some, well, a little scary. Her hand reached out. She unlatched the gate and pulled it open.

"Come here, you scamp."

What? She was inviting me into her yard? I was astamished. I couldn't believe this. But when she knelt down and patted a hand on her thigh and smiled, I knew it was true. With a yelp of sheer joy, I flew into her arms ... with a little too much oomph, I guess, because it knocked her over backwards into the grass.

Hey, I didn't care. Sally May wasn't a mean old hag, and I wanted the whole world to know it! She had smiled at me and invited me into her yard, and our relationship had been pulled back from the edge of the brink.

Fellers, I gave her the whole nine yards of Healing Licks, and we're talking about ears, cheeks, nose, neck ... every square inch of her lovely skin received the best licks money could buy. And instead of pushing me away, she pulled me into a loving embrace.

"Oh Hank, how can I stay mad at you? I know that deep in your heart, you want to be a good dog."

Oh, yes ma'am, the best dog in the whole world—just for you!

"But you're . . . you're such a dingbat."

Dingbat? I, uh, wasn't sure how to respond to that.

"Just promise me this." She held my face in her hands and looked deeply into my eyes. "Please stop barking at night. Please?"

I lifted my head to a Pose of Great Dignity. "All right, Sally May, if that's what it takes to patch up our relationship, I will promise—right here, today, in front of all these people—with Pete the Barncat and Dink the Parrot as my witnesses, I take a solemn oath never to bark again at night. Ever. Even if your husband orders the Security Division to bark at the moon, we will disobey orders. No kidding."

Pretty emotional occasion, huh? You bet. And that's about the end of the story. Sally May and I patched things up, I never barked again at night, and we lived happy ever afterly on the ranch.

This case is . . . wait, there's more.

CHAPTER TEN

I Give Pete a Crushing Defeat

The story should have ended there, but stories don't always stop where they're supposed to stop. So if you want the whole truth, we'd better keep going. Things might get a little shaky, but ... I can't reveal any more. What do you say? Stop here or run the risk of hearing the truth?

I agree. Let's take a deep breath and plunge on into the unknown.

Okay, right there in the backyard, Sally May and I healed old wounds and ended years of misunderstandings and bad feelings. She was in such a splendid mood that she allowed me to remain in the yard whilst she planted her bazoonia flowers. Putting on my very best behavior, I sat beside her for two solid hours and watched.

Guess who else was watching. Pete. Her precious kitty. I saw his cunning little eyes peeking out of the iris patch, and I could read his mind. He hated this! It ate his liver and gizzard that I had been invited to stay in the yard, and that I was sitting in the Position of Honor beside our beloved ranch wife.

He watched until he couldn't stand it any more. Out he came, purring and rubbing the paint off the side of the house. I'll admit that my ears leaped up and I felt a growl swelling in the depths of my throat, but with lightning reflexes, I began throwing switches and got everything shut down just in the nickering of time.

He gave me a haughty smirk, flicked his tail across my nose, and began rubbing on Sally May— and we're talking about rubbing the threads right off her blue jeans. He rubbed and purred, pranced and prissed, and missed no opportunity to beam hateful looks in my direction.

My finger twitched on the trigger of my mind, and you probably think that I launched the weapon and ruined everything. Nope. This time the cat had matched wits with an older dog, a wiser dog, a dog who had learned Life's Lessons the hard way.

Get this. I sat there like a granite statue made

of marble. I hardly moved a hair or a muscle, and I even gave the little fraud a pleasant smile.

Hee hee. It drove him crazy! There he was, using all his kitty tricks to get me inflamed, and I was ignoring him. That's the second-best thing you can do to a cat, don't you know. If circumstances don't allow you to beat him up and park him in a tree, ignore him.

Cats hate being ignored. It makes 'em purr louder and rub harder. They get careless and before long, they start making mistakes. Hee hee. Sally May was doing her very best to get the flowers in the ground (don't forget, she had people coming to a picnic), and kitty was crawling all over her like a boa constrictor.

She took it as long as she could. She gave him fair warning, but cats don't take hints. At last, Kitty Precious made the mistake of snapping off one of the flowers. Hee hee. It was delicious. Sally May leaped to her feet, snatched old Pete off the ground, and airmailed him back to his iris patch.

CRASH!

Wow, what a throw! She could have played shortstop on anybody's softball team.

Well, this was a very important event in ranch history. Do you see what it meant? *Someone besides me had pushed Sally May into a Volcanic*

Moment, and I felt that we needed to celebrate the occasion with a few rounds of Robust Barking.

"Hank, don't start that again!"

Or maybe not. As I've said before, it's often best to celebrate our little victories with a moment of, uh, silent meditation. Silently and meditatively, I recalled every delicious detail of Pete getting tossed . . . and loved every second of it!

Boy, life is good when the cats get in trouble.

At that moment, Loper came through the yard gate. "Hon, you'd better start getting ready."

She glanced at her watch. "I told everybody to come at six."

"Yeah, but you know Ken and Sandra: always early."

Sally May scowled. "They wouldn't dare."

"They're always early." His gaze drifted over to . . . well, to ME, it seemed. "What's Bozo doing in the yard?"

Sally May dusted off her hands. "Well, he's decided to become a good dog."

Loper laughed. "Miracles happen, I guess." He headed up the steps to the porch. There, he stopped and looked at Dink. "He is kind of pretty."

In a tender gesture, Loper extended his right index finger to rub the bird on its head. Dink bit him.

"Ow! Why you little ..." Loper snatched his finger away and turned to his wife. "If he ever bites me again ..."

She laughed. "Oh, you just don't have the right touch." She went up on the porch and started speaking baby-talk to the bird. "Him's a nice birdie. Him just doesn't like big ugly cowboys." She extended her right index finger to rub him on the head ... and Dink bit her, too.

Loper doubled up with laughter. "Him likes to bite, doesn't him?" Still laughing, he went into the house.

Sally May muttered something to the bird, then opened the gate and told me to leave the yard. I did, and she gave me a pat on the head. "Hank, you've been a good dog. When you do as you're told, we can get along just fine."

Yes ma'am. The hours we'd spent together, planting flowers, had restored my faith in ... well, just about everything: the human race, life, dogs, the world, relationships. Sally May and I had shared some precious moments together, and they would become our pattern for the future.

She headed for the house. On the porch, she paused and scorched the parrot with a stern glare. "If you ever bite me again ..." She went into the house to get ready for the company.

I stood there for a moment, warmed by the memories. Sally May adored me. At last she realized that cats are selfish, ungrateful little snots, and that parrots bite their friends. That left ... well, ME, you might say, to be her loyal companion through thick and thicker.

I heaved a sigh of satisfaction, turned, and headed back to the office. I had gone maybe twenty yards when I heard Sally May's voice. "Hank, I need your help. Will you please dig up those flowers?"

What? *Dig up the flowers?*

"Hank, come here!"

Yes ma'am.

I headed back to the yard gate, double-quick. I had some serious questions about her orders, and I mean SERIOUS questions, but now that we'd patched things up, I sure didn't want her doubting my loyalty. Don't forget her parting words to me: "Hank, when you do as you're told, we can get along just fine."

When I reached the yard gate, she was nowhere in sight. Dink sat on his perch and Pete's yellow eyes were peering at me from the iris patch.

Hmm. Sally May must have called out her message through the kitchen window. I did a quick scan and, sure enough, the window above the kitchen sink was open, but she wasn't there. What was the deal?

Hey, she'd spent most of the afternoon *planting* those flowers, working in the hot afternoon sun. I'd sat right there beside and watched the whole thing. It made absolutely no sense ...

"Hank, do as you're told!" Again, it was her voice.

My gaze leaped around, looking for her. Where was she? I'd heard her voice, loud and clear, but saw no sign of her. Did I dare enter her yard and begin the process of ...

Oooo boy, this didn't sound right. I mean, it sounded crazy. Dig up her flowers? For a moment, I was paralyzed. For one of the few times in my career, I had no idea what I should do.

Then a thought came to my mind. We had one witness in this case, a loafer who had been on the scene and whose testimony could set the record straight.

I took a deep breath and tried to calm my nerves. This wasn't going to be easy or pleasant. "Pete? Could we have a word?"

I know, I know. You should never build your case on the testimony of a cat, but what other choice did I have?

Pete slithered out of the iris patch and came rubbing down the fence. He was dawdling, taking his sweet time—exactly what you'd expect a cat to do in a moment of urgency. My wild instincts told me to scream at him, but I had to maintain a pleasant appearance.

He stopped about ten feet from where I was ... well, where I was boiling and about to explode. He gave me that smirk that drives me nuts and said, "Well, well! It's Hankie the Wonderdog. What brings you back to the yard?"

I was trembling all over. "Pete, I would rather eat worms than ask you for help, but ..." I swallowed hard. "I need your help."

"Ouch! That hurt, didn't it?"

"You'll never know how much. Okay, bottom line. You heard Sally May's voice, right?" He nodded. "Tell this court exactly what she said."

"She told you to dig up her flowers."

"See? That's what I heard, but it just doesn't make sense."

He sat there for a long time, drumming his claws and flicking the end of his tail. "Hankie, you're in this thing so deep, you don't even know which way is up."

"Explain that."

"It's the parrot, Hankie. He's playing you like a fiddle."

"The parrot! You're saying ..." I moved closer. "Forgive me for being suspicious, but why would you tell me that?"

"Not out of brotherly love, Hankie. Actually ..." He fluttered his eyelids. "I had a deal in mind."

"I've partnered with you on several deals, and I always get stung."

"This one will be easy." He leaned closer and whispered behind his paw. "You knock over the perch, and I'll eat the bird."

My mind was swirling. I marched a few steps away and tried to clear my thoughts. Then I whirled back to the cat. "Okay, it's all coming clear now. You and Drover are in this together, aren't you?"

"Drover? Not likely."

"He was the one who first planted this rumor that the parrot can talk."

"Drover is smarter than you think. So is the bird."

"Drover is a traitor, you are a little schemer, and the parrot is dumber than the perch he's standing on. Sorry, Pete, it won't work. You're dealing with the Head of Ranch Security, not chopped liver."

His gaze drifted up to the sky. "This is going to be very interesting."

"You bet. Now, step aside. I've got orders to dig up some flowers." I leaned toward him and added, "Orders from the same woman who pitched you across the yard. There, chew on that."

Heh heh. Told him, didn't I? You bet. I went into Deep Crouch, leaped over the fence, and marched straight over to the flowerbed. Behind me, I heard the parrot squawk, "Good doggie! Brave doggie! Awk!"

Hey, did you hear that? Maybe old Dink was smarter than I thought.

Company
Arrives

It had taken Sally May most of the afternoon to plant the flowers. You'll be proud to know that it took me only three minutes to unplant them. I mean, when you need serious backhoe work, call Hank the Cowdog.

Pete sat and watched the whole thing, wearing his usual smirk. When I was done, I pointed to my work and yelled, "There! That's what I think of you and your sneaky tricks."

Kitty seemed impressed. "Nobody puts on a better wreck than you, Hankie. I'm sure Sally May will be impressed."

"You bet she will. Now go chase your tail, before I ..."

At that moment, my ears picked up the sound of an approaching vehicle. I rushed to the north side of the yard and peered off into the distance. A white SUV had turned at the mailbox and was coming toward the house. The first of the picnic crowd had just hit the ranch.

Oh yes, in the process of doing this scouting work, I accidentally bumped into the cat and stepped on his tail. "Reeeer!" Tragic situation. Hee hee. I felt terrible about it. Old Pete shot me a killer look, snatched up his tail, and scampered back to the iris patch.

"Sorry, Pete. I guess I wasn't paying attention to my business."

Well, I had used up all the time we had allotted for cats and it was time for me to go into Escort and Greeting. A lot of your ranch dogs won't do E & G. I guess they figure that, because they're trained for cattle, any other kind of work is beneath their dignity.

Me? I've always tried to offer a broad package of services. I can work cows with the best of 'em, but I also do Traffic, Cats, Backhoe, Investigations, and, when the need arises, Escort and Greeting.

In this modern economy, a dog has to be versatile. When you get too proud of yourself, you can lose your job. Let's face it, dogs can be replaced. It happens every day.

So I dived over the fence and dashed around the north side of the house, arriving just in time to greet the first of our guests, Sandra and Ken Splawn. They were loyal members of the church choir. I'd heard it said that Mrs. Splawn had a lovely soprano voice, while her husband sang monotone.

Mrs. Splawn had gotten out of the car by the time I arrived, and was reaching into the back seat for a food dish she had brought. This gave me an opportunity to do a Scent Check on the legs of her blue jeans.

Hmmm. That was interesting. She owned a poodle. Did you realize that a highly trained dog can recognize the scent of a poodle? We can. They leave a distinctive signature, kind of a "town" smell, and most of your ranch dogs don't care for it. In fact, a lot of times we'll mark it out with a substance called Poodle Blocker.

I hoisted up my right hind leg and was about to . . .

"Don't you dare!"

Huh? Okay, some folks don't mind going around with poodle scent on their clothes. It's a big world and everybody's different. Me, I just try to fit in and get along.

Our guests had parked in front of the house and the picnic ground was down below the house, under those big elm trees. I led the way, choosing a route along the north side of the house.

As we were passing the backyard, the door opened and Sally May emerged, all fresh and clean and ready for the picnic. I gave her an adoring gaze and went to Broad Swings on the tail section.

She welcomed the Splawns to the ranch and noticed that Sandra was carrying a metal pan that was covered with alumimum foil... alunimum foil... covered with a strip of tin foil. "What did you bring?"

Mrs. Splawn said, "A chocolate sheet cake, my grandmother's recipe. It's yummy. I think you'll like it."

Chocolate cake? Is that what she'd said? I switched on Snifforadar and began pulling in air samples. Yes, by George, there it was, the heavy, creamy, bodaciously delicious smell of *chocolate*.

Have we discussed chocolate? Maybe not, because, well, we dogs very seldom get a chance to eat the stuff. I won't say that our people are too stingy to share it, but sometimes it appears that

way. But show me a normal, healthy American dog and I'll show you a dog that loves chocolate cake.

I, uh, went to Hydraulic Lift on the hind legs and hoisted my nose to the level of the pan in Mrs. Splawn's hands. Wow! I'd never met her grandmother, but I liked her already. You talk about a yummy chocolate smell!

Mrs. Splawn gave me a hard glare and said, "No!"

Me? Hey, I hadn't done anything. I was just checking things out. That was my job, after all.

Then she noticed Dink sitting on his perch and turned back to Sally May. "You bought a parrot?"

Sally May's face darkened. "We didn't buy it. Someone gave it to Loper, and we're not sure how we feel about that. It bit me this afternoon."

Dink seemed to be listening and he squawked, "Bought a parrot, bit the girl, chocolate cake!"

Sally May thought that was cute, and smiled, and she was about to say something when her gaze landed on the flowerbed.

Uh-oh. Right away, I knew we had a problem. I saw it written all over her face. She didn't have to say a word, but she said it anyway, and it was the word I had come to dread: my own name, screeched in an angry tone of voice.

"Hank!"

Oh brother. I had no idea what kind of crisis we had entered. My life with these people had taken on the pattern of a yo-yo. They were happy, they were mad, they were petting me, they were screeching. A dog never knew from one minute to the next whether he was a prince or a toad.

Sigh. Well, I didn't need to stick around for the rest of it. I already knew that, for reasons unknown, I gotten myself back on her List. I ducked my head, drew my tail up between my legs, and vanished behind a clump of sagebrush that happened to be growing nearby. There, I melted into the scenery and flinched at the howling voice that was coming from the porch.

"He destroyed my flowers! I spent all afternoon planting them and he dug them up, every last one of them! Disobedient hound! Where'd he go? Loper, you need to have a talk with your dog!"

You know, I like my people, I really do, but sometimes they just seem ... I don't know how to say this. Irrational, I guess. You follow their orders, then they blow a gasket and start screaming. First it was Loper, now Sally May.

The minutes passed. Sally May and the Splawns drifted down to the picnic ground. Other guests arrived and I could hear the sounds of laughter coming from down below. Everyone was having a wonderful time—pitching horseshoes, playing games, singing, talking.

Me? I was having anything BUT a wonderful time. It appeared that my career was over. I might as well pack up and move out, before this poisonous incident grew even poisonouser.

But then, as I was in the midst of the darkest of dark thoughts, something very unusual happened. I heard Sally May's voice, and you won't believe what she said. She said, "Hank, come down here and eat this chocolate cake!"

You probably think that I sprang to my feet and highballed it down to the picnic ground. I mean, most dogs don't need more than one invitation to eat a chocolate sheet cake, right? But I didn't move. See, the bond of trust between me and Sally May had been damaged beyond repair.

Might as well be honest. *I no longer trusted her.* Maybe she wanted to heal our wounds by giving me a chocolate cake, but what if I ate it and she changed her mind? It just wasn't worth the risk.

But then ... this will really shock you ... then I heard Loper's voice. "Hank, come eat this chocolate cake!"

Gee, they must have been feeling pretty bad about the way they'd treated me, and they *should* have felt bad. But I faced two difficult questions here. First, would one chocolate sheet cake heal all my wounds? And second, would I be mature enough to accept their apologies?

I rose to my feet and ... you have no idea what happened then.

You probably think I dropped everything, raced down to the picnic ground, collected my chocolate sheet cake, and wolfed it down.

No, that's not what happened. What happened was that I didn't do any of those things, and do you know why? *Because I didn't trust Loper either.* Had you forgotten about that nasty scene in the night? "Hank, get up here and bark at the moon!" And then SPLAT, a pitcher of cold water on top of my head.

No, as much as I would have loved to stick my face into Mrs. Splawn's chocolate cake, I just couldn't risk it. I sank back into the cover of the sagebrush and ...

Wait. Suddenly, I heard a third voice calling my name, and this time ... Slim? "Hank, get down here and eat this cake before we give it to the county clerk!"

CHAPTER TWELVE

The Villain
Is Exposed

County clerk? I didn't understand that part, but I was fluent in "cake." In fact, the very slurpen of it ... the very mention of cake opened up the waterworks of my mouth. But here's the very most important detail, and you probably missed it. I still trusted Slim.

Do you see how important that was? I mean, for those of us in Security Work, trust is everything. Without it, we're like ... something. A yard without a dog, a house without a home, a sandwich without bread, a picnic without flies, a germ without a child ... in other words, incomplete.

But on the other hand, I'd been sandbagged so many times in the past twelve hours, I wasn't sure who or whom I could trust anymore. I didn't even trust my own judgment. I needed the wise counsel of a friend. Where was Drover when I really needed him? Down at the picnic or hiding in the machine shed, so that left me with ...

You know, when a dog scrapes the bottom of the friendship barrel, he sometimes dredges up a cat. See, nobody likes cats, so if you give 'em a scrap of attention, they'll do almost anything. In other words, emotionally speaking, they work cheap.

So I found myself drifting back to the yard fence. I could see Pete's face framed by the green stalks of the iris plants. He was just sitting there, staring out at the world with his weird kitty eyes.

I cleared my throat and stared at the ground, searching for the proper words. "Uh ... Pete, you know that deal in the yard, when I stepped on your tail?"

"Yes."

"I've been thinking about that. I probably shouldn't have done it, and laughing about it was ... what can I say, Pete? It was pretty tacky, I can see that now."

"Uh huh. Is this an apology, Hankie?"

I flinched at the word. "It's similar to an apology, yes. Pretty close. Real close. Anyway, I was just thinking ... hey Pete, did you happen to hear Sally May calling me a while ago?"

"Yes."

"Was it really her voice?"

"No. It was the parrot."

"Pete, I still find that hard to believe."

He shrugged. "That's your problem, Hankie."

"Hmmm. Okay, a moment later, did you hear Loper's voice, calling my name?"

"Yes."

"Was it actually Loper's voice?"

"No. It was the parrot."

I beamed him a glare. "How can a parrot sound like two different people?"

"It's what parrots do, Hankie. He's very good at it."

I began pacing up and down the fence line. My mind was racing. "Okay, pal, that brings us to the crust of the crux. Tell this court, in your own words, did you then hear Slim calling my name?"

"Yes."

I stopped pacing and whirled around. "And tell this court . . . don't forget, you're under oath . . . tell this court, was it actually the voice of Slim?"

There was a moment of haunting silence. Pete smiled and said, "Yes."

"It really was Slim? It wasn't the bird?"

"That is correct."

"What if I think you're a scheming, lying,

cheating little crook of a cat? What if I don't believe anything you say?"

He shrugged. "I don't care. And you don't get any cake."

I licked my chops and pondered his words. "Pete, you and I have been through a lot together. I'll admit that sometimes I don't like you."

"My mother felt the same way."

"But you've really helped me at a time when I really needed help. I won't forget it, pal. One of these days, maybe we can find a little job for you in the Security Division."

"Oh my."

"Now, don't get your hopes too high. We're not talking about an executive job, but you know ... hauling trash, cleaning the office, something like that."

"Oh goodie."

"And as a bonus," I said with a wink, "what would you think if I left you a few crumbs of cake, huh? It's chocolate."

"Oh my, be still my heart!"

"Okay, well, I'm headed for the picnic ground. Give me about ten minutes, then come pick up your crumbs. And thanks again for your help."

"Any time, Hankie. It's always a business doing pleasure with you."

"Right, same here."

I left him in the iris patch and highballed it down to the picnic ground. I had to bite my lip to keep from laughing out loud. What a dunce! For a few crumbs of chocolate cake, he'd given me some incredibly valuable information. Hey, if he'd driven a harder bargain, I would have given him more than crumbs, maybe even half the cake.

And you know what? It would have been worth it. There's no upper limit on the value of good intelligence information. Whatever you have to pay—money, cake, gold, silver—it's worth it in the long run, because good information can be the difference between a huge success and a disaster.

If you can buy it for crumbs, heh heh, that makes the deal even sweeter, and the sweetest deal of all is to buy your information from a cat . . . on credit! Are you getting the picture? See, I'd paid nothing up front and had promised the little pest a few crumbs of cake. But what if I ate the crumbs myself and didn't pay off?

Hee hee! Well, why not? He was a little crook, and any time you can out-crook a crook, you've had a good day. Hee hee. Oh, I love sticking it to a cat!

Anyway, I headed down to the picnic ground and started looking for Slim, my trustworthy friend who had summoned me for the cake reward. I saw him at a distance. He was standing amidst a group of people who were singing. I paused and listened to the song:

> Because thy loving kindness is better than life.
> My lips shall praise thee, my lips shall praise thee.
> Thus will I bless thee while I live
> Thus will I bless thee while I live.
> I will lift up my hands in thy name.

Not a bad song, pretty good, in fact, but what else would you expect? These people were members of the church choir. But I had other things on my mind, better things than music. Cake. Chocolate sheet cake.

I made my way over to a line of tables, the tops of which were covered with pans, dishes, and trays that might have contained food. Sniff sniff. Yes, they did, and right away I began picking up the scents of fried chicken, roast beef, brisket, ribs . . . my goodness, this was quite a feast and I was kind of surprised that they had left it . . . well, unguarded, so to speak.

Not that they had anything to worry about while I was on the job. No sir. Okay, maybe I thought about poaching a few ribs and a slab of brisket, but when a guy gets into the higher ranks of Security Work, he has already learned to deal with temptation.

See, I'd been called out on a very specific mission and had been given a chocolate sheet cake, not brisket or ribs or fried chicken, so I walked past all those yummy smells until I came to the dessert table.

It was easy to find. Even Drover could have located a table that was groaning under the weight of cakes, pies, cobblers, and freezers of homemade ice cream.

I glanced around, looking for my pan of cake. It would have been better if Slim had taken it off the table and set it on the ground, where I could take care of my business without ... well, stepping in the other desserts. I mean, a dog can get into trouble, walking on pies and cobblers.

But I didn't find my cake on the ground. Would I wait for Slim to come and help? I gave that some thought and decided ... nah, he was busy with the guests and having a good time. I could find it myself. I would just have to be careful where I stepped.

Most of your ordinary run of ranch mutts would never have attempted this kind of maneuver, leaping up on a dessert table, but I was pretty sure that I had just the right combination of balance, athletic ability, and ... okay, I didn't notice the big pan of blackberry cobbler and, well, it had probably looked nicer without my paw prints on the crust, but a guy can't anticipate every little obstacle.

Anyway, once I was up on the table, finding Mrs. Splawn's cake was as easy as pie. (A little humor there: finding the cake was as easy as pie. Get it? Ha ha.) But the point is that if a dog has any kind of nose at all, finding a chocolate sheet cake is no big deal. And neither is stripping off the outer layer of tin foil. I got 'er ripped off and ...

Wow! WOW! This was like nothing I'd ever seen before—half an acre of chocolate cake! I mean, we're talking about the fillfullment of a dog's wildest dream.

Could I eat it all? Could any dog alive possibly devour three acres of chocolate cake? I didn't know, but by George, we were fixing to find out.

Some dogs think that you should approach a cake with dainty manners. Not me. I approached this one with all the finesse of a track hoe. A bulldozer. A snowplow. We're talking about eating a trench right through the middle of that rascal, and not looking back. No prisoners, no tomorrow, just chocolate cake forever.

Best cake I'd ever tasted. Outstanding. Mrs. Splawn's grandmother must have been a wonderful lady, because this cake was ...

"Hank! What on earth!"

Huh?

I looked up and glanced around. Two women stood in front of me. Sally May and Mrs. Splawn. Their faces showed ... well, I guess you'd have to say that they looked pretty surprised, finding a dog ... uh ... standing on the dessert table ... smeared with chocolate icing from one ear to the other ... with one foot in the blackberry cobbler and the other ...

This didn't look good.

Sally May's eyes grew wide. Her nostrils flared out. The skin on her face seemed to be turning, well, a dangerous shade of red. And remember those lines that appeared in her forehead when she was uncommonly mad? There they were.

Gulp.

A crowd had gathered: Slim, Loper, children, Little Alfred, people I didn't know. Loper's eyes rolled up inside his skull. Slim shook his head and looked up at the sky. Steam and lava were coiling out of Sally May's nose and ears.

Obviously, we had a misunderstanding. I switched on Looks of Remorse and tried to wag a message with my tail. "Hey, I know this looks bad, but Slim told me to eat the cake. Honest. No kidding."

I saw nothing but icy glares and faces of stone—except for Little Alfred, and he was grinning like a little monkey. But his grinning wasn't going to help me out of this deal. Fellers, I was in BIG TROUBLE.

But then ... pay attention, this is really amazing ... just then a voice in the distance broke the awful silence. It came from somewhere up near the house, and it said, "Hank, come down here and eat this cake!"

It was the voice of Sally May ... only she was standing right there beside me, and she hadn't said a word.

She was astonished. She stared at Loper and he stared at her. And then she gasped, "It's the parrot! He told Hank to eat the cake!"

Suddenly the people erupted in cries of laughter, and the story about Loper's parrot buzzed its way through the crowd. It was the high point of the whole evening, and the biggest laugh of all came when Loper yelled, "And Bobby Kile's going to get his bird back ... first thing tomorrow!"

Well, I was thrilled that nobody had stabbed me

through the heart with a plastic spoon or wrung my neck, and while they were enjoying laughter and fellowship, I saw no reason to waste the rest of the cake. I stuck my face into the pan and . . .

A lady leaned over in my direction. Hmm, Mrs. Splawn, and . . . well, she didn't look as pleasant as before. In fact, she growled, "Get out of my cake, you big oaf!"

Sure, no problem there. I had planned to thank her for the cake, but . . . maybe some other time.

I flew off the dessert table, grabbed a gear, and went into Deep Hiding. I mean, my people needed some time to sort through all the damage the stupid parrot had caused, and I was in no mood to push my luck.

When I emerged from exile two days later, most of the dark clouds had blown over. The morning after the picnic, Loper returned the parrot to the sheriff's department. Whether or not Dink ended up in a chicken pot pie, we don't know, but he had become Deputy Kile's problem, not ours.

Loper and Sally May had finally figured out that a talking bird had turned our ranch upside-down and turned friend against friend. He'd been the cause of my barking at the moon, digging up the flowers, and eating the cake. Sally May hugged

my neck and apologized and told me she regretted all the hateful things she'd said about me. Wow, what an emotional scene!

The part they didn't figure out was that Sally May's precious kitty had been involved in the scheme up to his ears, but that was okay. The little sneak hadn't fooled me, not even for a minute, and don't forget that Pete got no cake. Zero, not even a crumb.

Hee hee. There's the happy ending to our story. Once again, I had scored a huge moral victory over the cat, and had beaten him at his own shabby game.

Around here, it doesn't get any better than that.

This case is closed.

The following activities are samples from *The Hank Times,* the official newspaper of Hank's Security Force. Do not write on these pages unless this is your book. Even then, why not just find a scrap of paper?

"Photogenic" Memory Quiz

We all know that Hank has a "photogenic" memory—being aware of your surroundings is an important quality for a Head of Ranch Security. Now you can test your powers of observation.

How good is your memory? Look at the illustration on page 122 and try to remember as many things about it as possible. Then turn back to this page and see how many questions you can answer.

1. How many pies were there? 1, 2, 3, or 4

2. Which of Slim's feet was on the picnic table bench? His left or his right?

3. How many people were wearing glasses? 1, 2, 3, or 4

4. Was the ice cream maker's handle on the left or the right?

5. Was the person on the far right a man or woman?

6. How many of Hank's ears could you see? 1, 2, 3, or 17?

Rhyme Time

If Hank the Cowdog got his archenemy Pete the Barncat to leave the ranch, what would Pete do? Would he have to look for a job? What jobs could Pete do?

Example: Pete could open a sandwich shop and name it this: PETE'S EATS

1. Pete could be the commander of a bunch of boats.

2. Pete could be something found on your bed.

3. Pete becomes an echo and does this when you say something.

4. Pete becomes freezing rain.

5. Pete could become the computer key that gets rid of mistakes.

6. Pete becomes a farmer and plants this type of grain.

7. Pete invents some special kinds of Halloween candy.

8. Pete invents some new track running shoes.

9. Pete invents a secret handshake.

10. Pete could become the sun and make us feel this.

Answers:

1. Pete's FLEET
2. Pete SHEET
3. Pete REPEAT
4. Pete SLEET
5. Pete DELETE
6. Pete WHEAT
7. Pete's TREATS
8. Pete's CLEATS
9. Pete GREET
10. Pete HEAT

Eye-Crosserosis

I've done it again. I was staring at the end of my nose and had my eyes crossed for a long time. And you know what? They got hung up—my eyes, I mean. I couldn't get them uncrossed. It's a serious condition called Eye-Crosserosis. (You can read about the big problems Eye-Crosserosis caused me in my second book.) This condition throws everything out of focus, as you can see. Can you help me insert the double letters into the word groupings to create words you can find in my books?

DD	**NN**	**BB**	**UU**	**PP**	**DD**
EE	**LL**	**TT**	**FF**	**OO**	**GG**

1. SIY_____

2. PEY_____

3. ES_____

4. CHSE_____

5. MILE_____

6. KIING_____

7. DISAEAR_____

8. GD-BYE_____

9. BUERFLY_____

10. RUISH_____

11. VACM_____

12. STUING_____

Hank's PicWords

Hank and his friends made some PicWords that need to be unscrambled. Use the character name or item illustrated below. Then subtract the letters indicated from each name or word. Add what's left over together and the PicWord will be solved. Good luck!

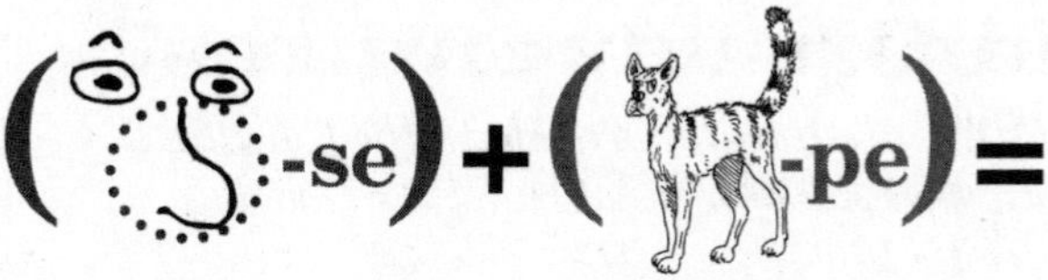

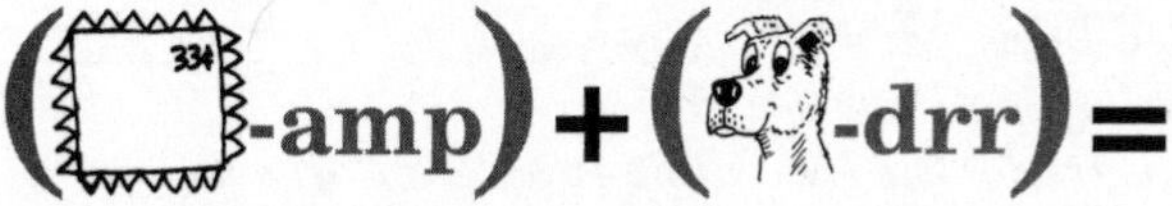

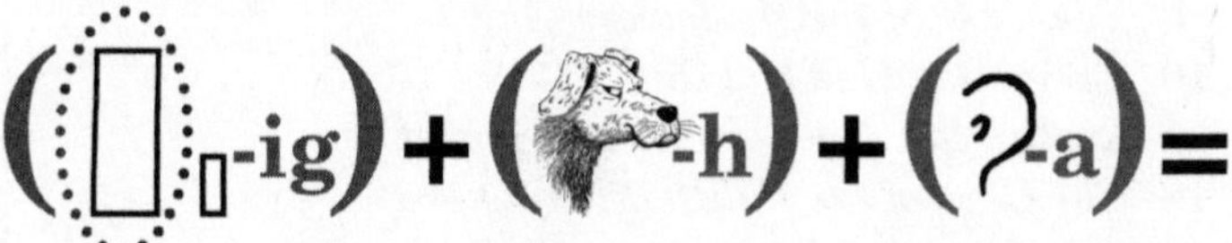

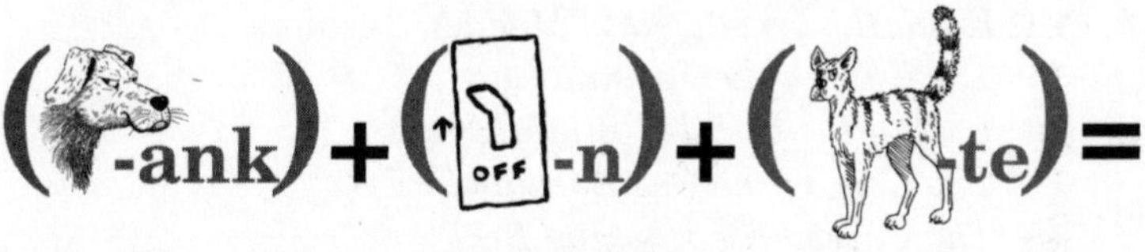

-se
-pe

334
-amp
-drr

-ig
-h
-a

-ank
OFF
-n
-te

Answers:

1. NOse + peTE = NOTE
2. STamp + drOVEr = STOVE
3. Big + hANK + EaR = BANKER
4. Hank + On + PEte = HOPE

Have you read all of Hank's adventures?

Join Hank the Cowdog's Security Force

Are you a big Hank the Cowdog fan? Then you'll want to join Hank's Security Force. Here is some of the neat stuff you will receive:

Welcome Package
- A Hank paperback of your choice
- A free Hank bookmark

Eight issues of *The Hank Times* with
- Stories about Hank and his friends
- Lots of great games and puzzles
- Special previews of future books
- Fun contests

More Security Force Benefits
- Special discounts on Hank books and audiotapes
- An original Hank poster (19" x 25") absolutely free
- Unlimited access to Hank's Security Force website at www.hankthecowdog.com

Total value of the Welcome Package and *The Hank Times* is $23.95. However, your two-year membership is **only $8.95** plus $4.00 for shipping and handling.

☐ Yes, I want to join Hank's Security Force. Enclosed is $12.95 ($8.95 + $4.00 for shipping and handling) for my **two-year membership**. [Make check payable to Maverick Books.]

Which book would you like to receive in your Welcome Package? Choose any book in the series.

(#   )   (#   )
_____
FIRST CHOICE   SECOND CHOICE

                                                 BOY or GIRL
_____
YOUR NAME   (CIRCLE ONE)

_____
MAILING ADDRESS

_____
CITY   STATE   ZIP

_____
TELEPHONE   BIRTH DATE

_____
E-MAIL

Are you a ☐ Teacher or ☐ Librarian?

Send check or money order for $12.95 to:

Hank's Security Force
Maverick Books
P.O. Box 549
Perryton, Texas 79070

DO NOT SEND CASH. NO CREDIT CARDS ACCEPTED.
Allow 4–6 weeks for delivery.

The Hank the Cowdog Security Force, the Welcome Package, and The Hank Times *are the sole responsibility of Maverick Books. They are not organized, sponsored, or endorsed by Penguin Group (USA) Inc., Puffin Books, Viking Children's Books, or their subsidiaries or affiliates.*